"The book is great and funny. It has a lot of adventure. I really liked it when Angela got to build the treehouse and spend time in it with her friends."

Owen, age 9 - Colorado

"The whole book was amazing! I really enjoyed the main character being introduced right away. The part about Kelly getting stuck was very amusing. One of my favorite parts was when they ran across the skunks."

Noah, age 14 – Tennessee

"The Treehouse was a good book. It made me want a treehouse, and a tire swing, and a see-saw, and cookies!!! There's never been a book that made me so jealous as this one."

Isaac, age 10 – California

"There is never a dull moment in this story. Every new chapter is fun and exciting! The crazy situations Angela and her friends get into bring back many fond memories of when I was a child and spent a lot of time in the woods behind our house. Now, even at 80 years old, I can relate to Angela's adventures and the relationships she has with her friends. Being a long-time friend of the author and her family, Paula was able to capture Angela's spunky personality and perseverance perfectly in this story. This book is fun, and funny, for any age!"

Pixie, age 80, Retired Librarian - Illinois

"Angela's story makes me want a treehouse. She was so happy to have it to sleep in and play in with Jeannie. It was funny when Kelly got stuck!"

Kate, age 6 1/2 - California

"Absolutely enjoyed reading this story myself and reading it to my grandkids! The author makes the pages come alive. I look forward to reading her next book."

Shelly, age 64, Retired – Illinois

"This book is great. It made me laugh out loud."

Annabelle, age 7 - Colorado

"This story is a page-turner! I couldn't put it down. I just couldn't wait to see what was going to happen next! This is an adventure that kids will really enjoy and remember. I almost cried when it ended because I wanted to read more!"

Janice, age 76 – Missouri

"In *Angela's Great Adventures: The Treehouse,* you'll join Angela and her group of friends as they work together to make her dream of a having a treehouse come alive. There's plenty of fun and action, along with some setbacks they must overcome.

"Author Paula Jo McElroy keeps the story moving with lots of funny incidents, lively dialogue, and tasty food to fuel the kids' big endeavor. She provides enough details about building the treehouse that it's almost a blueprint for building your own. This story is heartwarming and humorous, but also gives healthy lessons in family life, teamwork, consequences, and success.

"In a time of electronic overload, this is an excellent alternative that emphasizes physical outdoor activities. The story provides an excellent model for today's children, tweens, and young teens who may want to try a real-world challenge and experience the fun of being active."

Jerry Bingham, Ph.D, Professor of English & Writing - Illinois

"Let's get out of here!"

"What was that?" Jeannie said. She quickly turned her head and shifted her eyes toward the sound.

The kids strained to listen, as if their ears were high-powered radar listening devices. They looked in the direction of the sound, scanning the woods around them for any movement. Then it was quiet again.

Angela said in a soft voice, "Well, whatever it was, I don't hear it now. Let's keep going in case whatever it was is still out there."

The others nodded and moved slowly ahead, looking in all directions. About a dozen steps later, Jeannie said, "You guys... something's out there."

"I don't hear anything," said Jay.

Jeannie put her finger to her lips, "Shh." Then she whispered, "I'm telling you, something's out there. Listen!"

This time they all heard the rustling sound, and it sounded closer than before. The brother-sister duo slowly eased their load down to the ground in case they had to make a run for it. Angela's voice and finger trembled as she pointed to her left. "I just saw those bushes over there move."

Angela's Great Adventures

The Tree House

Book 1

Paula Jo McElroy

Illustrations & Cover Art by
Heather Sugg

Angela's Great Adventures: The Treehouse
Book One

ISBN: 979-8-218-51996-4

Printed in the United States of America

First Printing: 2024

PaulaJoMcelroy.com
paulajomcelroy@gmail.com

Illustrations and cover art by Heather Sugg

DEDICATION

To Angela, whose high-energy, fun-loving way gave
our family, and anyone who knew her, so many fun
memories. She was, and continues to be, a great
source of love, laughter, and enjoyment.

To my husband, Don. I cannot thank you enough for
your love and encouragement, as well as your input
and proofing throughout this writing journey.
Thank you for being my greatest fan!

CONTENTS

MEET ANGELA

Angela, also called Angie, is 12 years old. Most days you'll find her wearing old blue jeans and a hand-me-down t-shirt from her brother, quite often inside-out and backwards. Her hair is shaggy, her socks are baggy, and her smelly, dirty sneakers are usually untied. But what Angela wears most is a *great big smile*.

Angela isn't like most of the kids in her school; she likes being unique. She is kind, care-free, adventurous, untidy, and a faithful friend. Angela has a blended family, but to them they are simply *'family.'* Though much older than her younger siblings, she loves them and includes them in many of the things she does.

Angela's greatest goal in life is to have fun! Some of her favorite things to do include spending time with friends, exploring in the woods, skateboarding, roller skating/rollerblading, camping, playing video games, watching her favorite TV shows and movies, riding her motorized trail bike, and learning some Kung Fu moves from her big brother Brian. Angela especially enjoys great adventures – doing whatever and going wherever she can – even though her adventurous curiosity often gets her into a pickle... sometimes, even a little trouble.

"The more excited Angie is, the bigger her eyes get and the faster she talks, but my 80-year-old ears can't listen that fast!" – Grandma G.

MEET THE OTHER CHARACTERS

Jeannie, and her brother Jeremy, live next door to Angela at the end of the cul-de-sac. She is the same age and height as Angela, is always happy to help others, and is the voice of reason in the group for doing what is right. Jeannie has short blonde hair with large curls, blue eyes, and a cute round face with tiny freckles across her nose and cheeks. Jeannie is more like a mom than a tomboy, but she loves going on adventures with Angela.

Jeremy (9) is Jeannie's shadow. He goes nearly everywhere Jeannie goes and likes hanging out with the older kids. Jeremy is a mini-version of his father – he's smart, determined, and hard-working. His mom fondly calls him, and his dad, "Weasel-Butt" because they are skinny with no backside to hold up their pants – like a weasel or ferret. Jeremy has blue eyes and straight blonde hair that stands up a little in the back.

Jay (11) lives across the street from Angela. He has thick, brown hair that's hidden by a baseball cap. Jay's new eyeglasses somewhat hide his beautiful, nearly clear sky-blue eyes that stand out against his dark skin that looks suntanned all-year long. Jay is carefree, funny, and easy to get along with. He is rarely in a hurry and has but one speed – slow and steady. He's tall for his age and a little on the pudgy side. Like Jeannie, Jay is always ready to join Angela on one of her fun adventures.

Kelly (13) is only about six months older than Angela. He lives down the street, just across the street from the bus stop. Kelly used to hang out with Angela and the others, but now that he's going into middle school, he doesn't spend much time with them. Instead, Kelly spends most days on his electronic devices and playing video games with his so-called "friends online."

Brian is Angela's 16-year-old big brother. Brian is fun, smart, caring, and adventurous. He's also a bit of a daredevil – he's not afraid to try something new. Brian loves Angie, and is protective of her, but he also has fun teasing her and pulling jokes on her. He has a cool car, a black belt in the martial art of Kung Fu, plays the guitar, sings, and works a summer job; yet somehow he finds time to hang out with his friends and his family.

Sarah (5) is Angela's adorable little sister. She is sweet, loving, kind, shares well with others, and is always happy to help her mom in the kitchen. She has long brown hair that lays in large curls and big brown eyes. She loves her family and is like a protective little mom of her younger brother Matt.

 Matthew (3), called Matt or Matty, is Angela's little brother. He is very cute, with brown hair and big brown eyes like his sisters, and giggles like a little chipmunk. He is curious, loves his family, and mimics nearly everything Sarah says and does.

Sarah and Matty adore their big sister. They're like "three peas in a pod" – they love being together whether they're playing a game or snuggling up to watch a movie. Sarah and Matty aren't old enough to go on adventures with the older kids yet, but they love that Angela includes them whenever she can.

 Casey is the family dog. He loves his family, and he is one of Angela's best friends. Casey looks at Angela and listens to her as if he understands every word she says. Casey is a nine-month-old, 85-pound golden retriever puppy – a big one! He has gigantic paws, a long tongue that gives wet, sloppy kisses, and a happy tail that wags so hard it makes his hips sway and really hurts when it hits your legs! Casey gets excited around his family and often goes on what they call a hyper-run. Though large, he's still a clumsy puppy who can't always stop in time and sometimes knocks Angela down.

Now, come along on one of Angela's Great Adventures!

CHAPTER 1

School's Out for Summer

Angela couldn't wait for her noisy school bus to turn into her subdivision. The kids were rowdier than normal as they celebrated the last day of school. Angela liked school, but she liked summer break more. She daydreamed about the fun adventures she and her friends might have during her ride home.

Suddenly, Angela raised her arms over her head and shouted, "School's out for summer!"

A loud cheer filled the bus as it bumped and swayed down the road. The brakes on the long yellow school bus squeaked loud as it came to a halt at the end of Angela's street. She scooted off the edge of her seat and jetted down the aisle ahead of her friends. She waited behind the line on the floor for the bus driver to turn on the flashing red warning lights and push the handle to flip out the "STOP" sign before opening the doors. With her backpack in place, she gripped the handrail as she prepared for her swift exit.

"Hold on a minute." the bus driver said. "Let me do my job."

Angela was filled with excitement from the top of her head to the bottom of her feet. Even Angela's hair was excited for summer vacation! Angela felt like the driver was moving at a snail's pace.

Then, *SWOOP – SQUEAK – BANG*, the bus doors slapped open.

Angela flew over the three bus steps in one big leap, like an Olympic long jumper, landed safely on her feet, and trotted down the street toward home. Then she turned around and waved to the bus driver, "Thank you!"

The driver waved. "You're welcome! Have a great summer!"

Angela smiled and waved, then shouted to her friends, Jeannie, Jeremy, and Jay, who had just stepped off the bus, "I'll phone you later and we'll do something fun!"

"Like what?" they asked.

Angela, with her arms opened wide, shrugged her shoulders and shouted, "I don't know… but it'll be fun!"

Angela ran up her gravel driveway and scaled the steps in huge leaps, missing every other step. She threw open the door, dropped her backpack, and kicked off her sneakers.

"Mom. I'm home!" Angela charged like a bull to the kitchen for a snack and a quick hello-hug. Her mom smiled as her energetic daughter rattled on about the last day of school.

"Boy, am I hungry! I thought today would never end. Can I have a snack? Oh, and you wouldn't belie-e-e-eve what happened today! Is it okay if I play with my friends after my snack? What time will Dad be home tonight? Do you think I could…"

"Angie," her mom said. "Angela! Take a breath!"

Angela laughed when she realized she'd been talking non-stop at high speed ever since she came in the door.

"To answer your questions…yes, you may; really; yes; and, as usual, your dad will be home at six o'clock. Now, eat your snack so you can go out and play."

Angela smiled, then took a huge bite of her brownie and tucked it inside both of her cheeks. She looked like a cute little chipmunk storing away food for winter. Before sitting down to eat the rest of her snack, Angela fetched her backpack from beside the front door and set it down beside her chair. She took another bite of brownie, then unzipped her backpack and pulled out a beat-up, well-used spiral notebook and a pencil that had been sharpened down to a two-inch nub. Angela flipped past the pages of history, geography, and science notes; past the oodles of doodles; until finally finding a clean page to write on. Angela doodled a lot because of her ADHD – *Attention Deficit Hyperactivity Disorder*.

But now her full focus was on the empty page. She picked up the pencil nub and wrote **'My Summer Adventure List'** in large letters at the top of the page. She took another bite of brownie. *Hmm…what to do first,* she thought. *Well, I like watching TV, playing video games, and watching funny videos online.* Then, Angela reasoned with herself. *No, I need to save those things for rainy or super-hot days, or when I'm alone or don't have anything better to do.* In between bites, Angela made a long list of fun things she and her friends might do during their summer break. Angela smiled as she underlined the last item. Then she thought, *Today's the day I ask Mom and Dad if they will build me a treehouse. That would make my entire summer better.*

"You're unusually quiet," her mom said. "What are you up to?"

"I'm making a list of fun things to do this summer – you know, like skateboarding, camping out, going on the trails and other stuff.

My Summer Adventure List

1. Go exploring in the woods

2. Skateboarding

3. Go Hiking and Camping

4. Watch tv — Play video games —Watch movies
   (only on rainy or super hot days)

5. Have a lemonade stand

6. Ride trail bike on the trails

7. Swimming and Tubing

8. Stay up late and sleep late

9. Ride my bike

10. Sleepovers with friends

11. Play on the Slip n Slide

12. Go Roller Skating at the rink

13. Ride horses at the Ritchie's farm

14. BUILD A TREEHOUSE!!!

Her list now complete, Angela laid her stubby pencil down and carefully tore the page from her notebook. She grinned as she read the list of adventures. *I can always add more things later,* she thought. She grabbed the notebook and crammed it into her bulging backpack. Then, deciding the pencil nub still had some life in it, she dropped it in as well.

"Take your backpack to your room before you go out to play," her mom said from the kitchen. "Make sure you take out anything that shouldn't be in there all summer long."

"Okay," Angela said. She closed the backpack zipper just enough to keep the contents from spilling out, then slung the heavy backpack over her shoulder, and hurried up the steps to her bedroom. Angela didn't want to take the time to clean out her backpack. So in her hurry to go out and play, she flung open her closet door and heaved the heavy pack in to join the other stuff piled in her closet.

"I'll deal with you later," Angela said to the backpack while closing the door. Unfortunately, Angela forgot about the half-eaten peanut butter sandwich and two hard-boiled eggs hiding out in the bottom of her bag.

Before going out to play, Angela taped the Summer Adventure List to her closet door and smiled. Then, she kissed the palm of her hand with a loud smack and stuck the kiss to the last item on the list… 14. BUILD A TREEHOUSE! She held her palm against the list for a second while making a wish. Then she bolted for the stairs, her feet thundered down the open wooden steps.

"I'm going outside now," Angela said. She shoved her feet into her shoes but didn't tie them because that would take way too long.

"Alright. I'll call you when supper's ready," her mom said. "And tie your shoes!"

Angela whined, "Okay." She stopped just long enough to tie her shoes and then joined her friends on the cul-de-sac in front of her house to tell them about her *Adventure List* – especially her wish for a treehouse.

CHAPTER 2

A Glorious Treasure

Being outdoors made Angela happy – the sun on her face, the birds, the animals, and the creepy-crawlies like lizards, frogs, insects, and even the *friendly* snakes that lived in the woods around her neighborhood. But she didn't like centipedes or millipedes! All their little legs made her skin crawl and her legs run away.

Even though Angela didn't know what she might find along the way, each day brought a new adventure to embark upon, whether by herself or with her good friends, Jeannie, Jeremy, and Jay.

Jeannie, and her brother Jeremy, live next door to Angela at the end of the cul-de-sac. Jeannie is the same age and height as Angela. She is a nice girl who is always happy to help others, and she is the voice of reason in the group of friends to do what is right. She has long legs, short blonde hair that lies in large curls, pretty blue eyes, and a cute round face with tiny freckles across her nose and cheeks. Jeannie is more like a mom than a tomboy, but she loves going on adventures of any kind with Angela.

Jeremy is three years younger than Angela and is Jeannie's shadow. He goes nearly everywhere she goes, and he likes hanging out with the older kids. Jeremy is a mini-version of his father – smart, hard-working, and determined. His mom fondly calls him, and his dad, "Weasel-Butt" since they are skinny with almost no backside to hold up their pants – like a weasel or ferret. Jeremy has blue eyes and blonde hair like his sister, but his hair is straight and stands up a little in the back.

Jay is one year younger than Angela, and lives across the street from her. He has thick brown hair that is usually hidden beneath a baseball cap. Jay's eyeglasses somewhat hide his beautiful sky-blue eyes that stand out against his dark skin that looks suntanned all-year long. Jay is carefree, funny, and easy to get along with, but he is rarely in a hurry and has but one speed – slow and steady. He's tall for his age and a little on the pudgy side. Like Jeannie, Jay is always ready to join Angela on one of her fun adventures.

Angela and her family were new to the small northern town with a whopping population of 1,800 people. Uprooted from the only place she'd ever called home, Angela was now 800 miles away from her childhood friends and her extended family. She was an outsider and having a difficult time fitting in at her school. Most of the kids in her new, much smaller school already had friends they had grown up with. The city kids tended to hang out with their city kid friends; the farm kids with their farm kid friends; and the country kids with their country kid friends. They didn't need Angela, especially since she was different than most of them.

On Sundays, most of the kids in her small school attended the large, prominent, church on the hill at the south end of Main Street. But Angela's family attended the small church at the north end of Main Street.

Angela thought most of the kids in her school talked with a funny northern accent; they thought Angela talked with a funny southern accent. That seemed strange to her since she was from the heart of the Midwest in central Illinois where most of the people didn't talk with any accent.

Angela felt like an outsider. She didn't live in town; she didn't live in the country; or on a farm. Their neat log home was in a small wooded subdivision across the river, just a mile or two from the edge of town. But, as luck would have it, most of the kids around her age in the neighborhood were also outsiders. Like Angela, they were transplanted to the area because of their father's jobs. Angela, Jeannie, Jeremy, and Jay were each unique in their own ways, but they quickly became friends. Together they made a great team – a band of misfits who loved adventure.

For three years Angela dreamed of having a treehouse. She longed for a special place to play, sleep, and hang out in.

That night at dinner with her family, Angela clasped her hands in her lap and pressed her lips together as she thought of how to ask her parents for a treehouse.

She looked to her left and said in a timid voice, "Mom…"

Then she looked to her right and said, "Dad…"

Angela's chest swelled as she breathed in a deep breath, then she blurted out, "Can I *please* have a treehouse? I'm old enough now. I will help build it and I promise to take good care of it and play in it *all* the time! *Ple-e-e-ease*, can I have a treehouse?"

Her dad crossed his arms as he thought about it. He remembered how much fun he had playing in the treehouse his father had built for him when he was young. He sat in silence, and even though he was smiling on the inside, he greatly enjoyed watching Angela squirm in suspense. She was impatient and she usually wanted things *right now*.

Angela broke the silence. "If it'll help, I know where there's a pile of old lumber in the woods that we can use. I found it last year when I was exploring."

One year earlier, Angela found an old junk pile while trekking through the woods. She decided it was *"finders' keepers"* since there were no signs of anyone living nearby. She dug through the heap, hoping to find some worthwhile trinkets, while keeping an eye out for any unfriendly creepy-crawlies that may have made their home there. Her digging turned up some interesting things, but mostly she found a lot of junk. From the looks of things, the pile had been there a long time.

Angela moved things around with a stick she found along the trail. Suddenly, something moved! She jumped back, but kept her gaze fixed on the pile. Angela looked around her and picked up a stone that just fit her hand. Then, focusing her eyes on where the sound came from, she drew back her arm and hurled the rock into the rubble. Scared from its home, something long and black with a bright green stripe down its back slithered out. Angela screamed and jumped back again. She thought about running away, but then she saw that it was merely a harmless garter snake, and watched as it quickly disappeared into the thick underbrush.

Angela let out a huge sigh of relief and resumed her digging. She made sure to keep a watchful eye out for anything else that called the pile its home. Angela unearthed a few old glass bottles of assorted sizes and styles, including a pint-sized milk bottle from an old dairy farm, some antique teaspoons, a metal drinking cup, some old bottle caps, and two broken porcelain figurines. Though encased in dirt, everything she found was a treasure to Angela.

After a while, Angela took a break from digging and sat back on her heels. A slight smile crossed her face as she breathed in the beauty surrounding her. Then she spied something through the trees that captured her attention. She hopped to her feet and ran through the ocean of ferns, stopping just short of it. She stepped closer. Her mouth dropped open. Then, as if the trees and ferns had ears, Angela hollered with her arms stretched wide, "My treehouse!" She gazed in disbelief at a beautiful heap of old lumber.

She walked around the pile, believing that one day it might be used to build her treehouse.

Angela returned to the junk pile. She stuck her hands in the front pockets of her jeans and wiggled her fingers around to check for holes. *Good. No holes*, she thought. She put the teaspoons, bottle caps, and porcelain doll figurines in her pockets. Then she gathered up the front of her baggy t-shirt to form a pouch for the larger items. When Angela got home, she washed and dried her loot, then displayed the items on her bedroom windowsill like priceless works of art.

Now, nearly a year later, Angela was using that glorious pile of old lumber as a bargaining tool to influence her parents' decision about building her a treehouse.

Still sitting at the dinner table, Angela's parents looked at each other; only their eyes were speaking. Angela wished she could hear what they were talking about. They raised their eyebrows and tilted their heads saying…

What do you think?

I don't know. Is it time for a treehouse?

Maybe. She would have a lot of fun with a treehouse.

Finally, her dad said with a straight face, "Well… maybe."

"*Really?*" Angela bounced in her chair with excitement.

"Maybe," her mom and dad said again with firm voices.

"We will discuss it and let you know. Go outside and play while we talk it over."

The excitement drained from Angela's face. She loosened the grip she had on the sides of her chair and slouched. "Okay," she said in a low voice. She stood up slowly, hung her head, and shuffled her feet toward the door. Once outside, Angela thought, *well...they didn't say no.* Then she smiled a little smile, crossed her fingers on both hands and then laid her arms across her chest. She would have crossed her eyes if she thought it would help. Then Angela closed her eyes and made a wish.

"Please let them say yes to a treehouse this time."

CHAPTER 3

Exciting News!

Angela ran to tell her dog, Casey, about the treehouse. She wrapped her arms around his neck and gave him a squeeze. The force of Casey's wagging tail made his hips sway. Then Angela held his head in her hands, and sitting nose to nose, she said, "Guess what, Casey? I might be getting a treehouse!" He gazed at her as if he understood every word, and then gave her a wet, sloppy kiss across her face. Angela stroked Casey's beautiful reddish coat and talked to him for what seemed like an hour as she waited.

Just then Angela's mom stuck her head out the door and said, "Angie, you can come inside now." Angela sprang to her feet and sprinted like a gazelle toward the house; her feet barely grazed the steps. She tripped on one of her shoelaces but caught herself on her hands before falling.

"Whew! That was a close one!" Angela said over her shoulder to Casey. Then she stopped, took a deep breath, and went inside. She stood in front of her parents; she looked first at one, and then the other. Angela couldn't stand the deafening silence.

"Well?" She paused. "Can I have a treehouse?" Her legs jiggled as she awaited their answer.

Her parents just stood there – silent – arms crossed – straight faced. The suspense was nearly more than she could bear.

"Aaaah!" Angela growled. "You guys are driving me crazy! Well? Do I get to have a treehouse?"

"We wonder if you're old enough to handle that responsibility, plus there's the cost of building a treehouse."

"But I'm twelve now, and I found all that lumber in the woods that we can use so you don't have to buy very much."

Her parents looked at each other, smiled, then raised their arms and said, "You're getting a treehouse!"

Angela jumped into her dad's arms. "Thank you, Dad!" Then she hugged her mom. "Thank you! Thank you! Thank you!"

"However," her dad said, "you will have to help us build it."

"Yes, of course, I will," she said, jumping up and down. "I've got to tell Jeannie and Jay. Can I call them?"

"Go ahead," her mom said.

Angela ran to phone Jeannie.

"Jeannie, I have great news! Can you meet me in front of my house? I'm going to call Jay too."

"Hang on. Let me ask my mom. I'll be right back." Jeannie returned less than a minute later. "I'll see you in a few minutes!"

Then Angela had the same conversation with Jay, who, after checking with his mom, said, "I'll be right over!"

Then Angela told her mom, "I'm going outside now to tell Jay and Jeannie about the treehouse!"

"Alright. Come in when the streetlight comes on," her mom said.

"Okay!" Angela said, then raced out the door.

Angela met Jay just as he was crossing the street, and Jeannie as she was reaching the end of her long driveway. Just then they heard the screen door slam at Jeannie's house. They turned around to see Jeannie's shadow running down the driveway as fast as he could go. Jeremy wasn't going to miss out on the news! They huddled around Angela as she told them about the treehouse. Her excitement was contagious. She told them about retrieving the old lumber from the pile in the woods; everyone was happy to help.

Then Jay said, "Maybe we should ask Kelly if he wants to help. He used to hang out with us all the time."

Kelly is about six months older than Angela and lives at the opposite end of the street across from the bus stop. Now that he's going into middle school, he spends most of his time playing on his electronic devices; watching online videos, social media, and playing video games with his so-called "friends online."

Jeannie huffed and rolled her eyes. "Why bother?" she said. "All he does is play video games and mess around on the internet."

Jeremy nodded. "Yeah. Kelly doesn't care about us anymore. He just sits in his room playing on all his *stupid devices* and he's getting fat and lazy."

"That wasn't very nice to say," Angela said in a firm voice. Then she pointed her finger at Jeremy, saying, "Kelly's a nice guy; he's still our friend; and you shouldn't talk about him like that!"

"Hey, he's nine," Jeannie said, defending her brother. "I agree with Angela; Kelly *is* a nice guy. But, Jeremy's right too. Kelly has changed. I'm not being mean – just honest. Kelly never wants to do anything with us anymore, and frankly, we're tired of asking him."

Jay shrugged his shoulders and said, "*Maybe* Kelly is this way *because* we don't ask him. It goes both ways, you know."

The kids shifted their eyes down to the pavement as they quietly processed Jay's words.

"That's it!" Angela said. "We're marching down there right now to ask him! And maybe, like Jay said, Kelly just needs to know that we're still his friends and we care about him."

"Yeah," said Jay. "Let's go!"

So, the gang whirled around and walked shoulder-to-shoulder down the center of the street like a posse in pursuit toward Kelly's and lined up the same way on his front porch facing the door.

Then Angela said, "Let *me* do the talking since it's my project."

Everyone nodded, Angela pressed the doorbell button, and they waited. The silence was broken by the sound of Kelly's little dog's yapping and the rhythmic sound of footsteps pounding toward the door. They recognized the sound of Kelly's voice when he scolded the dog from behind the door.

"Stop that! Be quiet!" he said.

Kelly yanked the door open. He was unprepared to see his four friends standing on his porch, especially since it had been a while since they'd come to see him *for anything*. He had a puzzled look on his face, his noisy little fluff-ball dog cradled in one arm, and an unopened bag of chips and a soft drink in the other.

"Uh... hi, you guys. What are you doing here?"

Angela stood tall and stated her case in one long breath.

"My mom and dad are gonna build me a treehouse and there's a pile of old lumber in the woods that we're gonna bring to my house to build it with and we wanna know if you want to do it with us cuz it's gonna be a lot of fun whadayathink?"

Kelly stared wide-eyed at Angela during her non-stop speech. Her babble left him frozen and speechless.

Jay broke the ice. He pointed to Angela and said, ""Yeah, what she said. Do you want to help us?"

Kelly felt as though he were standing before the school principal. His eyes scanned their expectant faces while his mind searched for reasons to *not* help them. "Hmm. Well... thanks for thinking of me, but I don't know. Umm... It's pretty hot outside, and that sounds like hard work. I don't usually get up until around noon, and my mom said I have to take out the trash and clean my room tomorrow before I can do anything else or play my video game. I'm on a real hard level that I'm trying to beat." He was running out of excuses.

Jeremy spouted off but was quickly shushed by his sister.

"See, I told ya..."

"Shh!" Jeannie gave her brother the stink-eye of disapproval.

Angela quickly reached out and patted the little dog's head to distract Kelly's attention away from Jeannie and Jeremy.

"Well, c'mon down tomorrow morning about nine if you change your mind," Angela said.

"Alright. I'll think about it," Kelly said, and then closed the door.

Jeannie threw her arm around Jeremy and cupped her hand over his mouth to keep him quiet until well out of Kelly's hearing range.

Jeremy jerked free and scowled at her. "What'd you do that for?"

"I didn't want you to open your big mouth and hurt Kelly's feelings. I never know what you're going to say."

"Well, just don't do that again!" Jeremy said. Then he walked off in a huff, swinging his skinny little arms back and forth with each pounding step.

"I guess I made him mad," Jeannie said.

"Look at him go," Angie said.

"Yeah, he can really fly when he's mad!" said Jay.

"Honestly," Jeannie said, "Jeremy isn't *mad* at Kelly. He likes him, and he says those things because he misses doing things with him. Jeremy thinks Kelly doesn't hang out with him because he did something wrong, or that he's too little now that Kelly's going into middle school. I told Jeremy that people change when they grow up, that he didn't do anything wrong, but he doesn't believe me."

"We all miss Kelly," Angela said, "and I'm glad we went down there, even if he did say no. We're not giving up on him."

Jeannie and Jay agreed, and the trio continued toward home.

Angie waved and turned into her driveway. "See you guys in the morning."

Just then the streetlight came on.

"Well, that was good timing," Jay said.

"Eat a good breakfast. You're gonna need it!" Angela hollered.

"Okey-dokey," Jeannie said.

"Yes, *Mom*," Jay said in a fun, sarcastic tone.

Jay and Jeannie walked their separate ways, waving goodbye over their heads without turning around.

Angela was afraid she'd be too excited to sleep, but after a warm shower she soon drifted off to la-la-land.

CHAPTER 4

The Recovery Mission

The trio of friends arrived at Angela's house after breakfast the next morning. *Ding-dong!* Angela's mom greeted them at the door. "Good morning kids. C'mon in."

Angela's little sister Sarah (5) and brother Matt (3), nicknamed Matty, were sad because they weren't old enough to go on the adventure with the big kids. But that changed when Angela told them they could help decorate the treehouse when it was finished.

"Yay!" they shouted, clapping and jumping up and down.

"Sarah, can we use your wagon to carry the boards?"

Sarah and Matty, always happy to share, shouted, "Yes!"

It was a beautiful, sunshiny day with a bright blue cloudless sky. The friendly foursome was dressed for hard work and ready to set out on their first adventure of the summer. Angela even tied her shoes – extra tight this time. The big kids filed out the back door and down the steps to begin their journey.

"Be careful and have fun!" Angela's mom said from the porch.

"Be careful!" Sarah and Matty repeated. "Have fun!"

"Okay. We will!" they said.

The fearless foursome fell into place with Angie in the lead, followed by Jeannie, then Jeremy, with Jay in the rear, pulling the little red wagon behind him across the cul-de-sac. Watching the pep in their steps and listening to their cheerful voices as they disappeared into the stand of tall pines, oaks, and ferns made Angela's mom smile. Though the foursome was no longer visible, Angela's mom and the kids could hear them singing a fun song.

"I'm bringing home a baby bumblebee,
Won't my mommy be so proud of me,
I'm bringing home a baby bumblebee,
Ouch! It stung me!"

The kids laughed and sang louder than before.

"I'm squishing up the baby bumblebee,
Won't my mommy be so proud of me,
I'm squishing up the baby bumblebee,
Ooh! It's yucky!"

"I'm licking up the baby bumblebee,
Won't my mommy be so proud of me,
I'm licking up the baby bumblebee,
Mmm. He's yummy!"

"You guys are so gross!" Jeannie said.

Angela and the boys burst into laughter. Jeannie resisted, but then joined in. Their chatter, singing and laughter soon became a distant noise, and then, silence.

Angela led the pack of friends down the narrow well-packed trail formed by the many trips she and her friends had made during their hikes into the woods. They resembled a freight train gliding down the tracks. Angela was the engine, the driving force; Jeannie, Jeremy, and Jay were the freight cars behind the engine; and the wagon was the bright red caboose. The rhythm of their eight feet pounding on the trail was like the chugging sound of a train... CHUGA-chuga, CHUGA-chuga, CHUGA-chuga, CHUGA-chuga. Their occasional burst of laughter was like the train's steam whistle. The soft ferns along the trail waved back and forth in their wake.

The kids left the trail and waded through the knee-deep ocean of soft, wild ferns that grew in the shade of the tall oaks to retrieve the treasure of unclaimed lumber from its hiding place. When they reached the treasure heap, they immediately got to work pulling the boards from the pile and stacking the best ones neatly on the wagon. They made several trips in and out of the woods, hauling what they could safely handle – one small wagon-full at a time – past patches of poison ivy and prickly thorn bushes along the way.

Though determined to complete their mission by the end of the afternoon, the kids were ready for a break. They returned with a load and were surprised to find a picnic lunch Angela's mom had set up for them on the back porch. The hungry kids quickly inhaled the peanut butter and jelly sandwiches, chips, grapes, and carrot sticks, and then slurped down a big cup of icy cold lemonade.

Jay took another bite of his sandwich, and said, "I wish Kelly would have come." Then he spread his arms wide and said, "Look what he's missing out on – sunshine, blue skies, fresh air, beautiful scenery, and a fun time with great friends."

Jeremy smiled and patted Jay and Angela on the back. "That's right," Jeremy smiled and said, "especially a great friend like me!"

"And don't forget about our marvelous singing!" Jeannie said.

"Yeah, we should go on tour!" Jay said. Then he noticed a glob of jelly on his hand. "Look – I'm licking up a baby bumblebee..."

Everyone laughed when Jay pretended to lick up a squished bee from his hand. The others followed his example by doing the same – all except Jeannie. She made a face like she had just bitten into a sour lemon.

"You guys are disgusting!" she said.

"Oh, we're just having fun," Angela said. "C'mon, let's get back to work before we're too tired to move."

The kids carried their plates and cups inside.

"Thanks for the lunch, Mom," Angela said.

"Yeah, thanks for lunch, Mom," the others echoed, smiling.

"You're welcome. I'm glad you enjoyed it."

One by one, the kids jumped off the porch and headed for the woods with the little red wagon in tow. Back at the wood pile, they attacked the dwindling treasure heap with renewed energy.

"I sure hope there aren't any critters living in this woodpile," Jay said, pulling another board from the heap.

"Me too," said Jeannie.

"Me three!" said Jeremy.

"Me four!" said Angela.

"I'm going to work on the other side," Jay said. After pulling a couple of boards from the pile, he said, "Whew, something smells over here! It looks like there's a nest or something under these boards!"

The others ran around the pile to see the nest. Jeannie kneeled down to get a closer look and, unfortunately, a good whiff of the strong odor too.

"Ooo-eee! It does stink!" Jeannie stood up and pinched her nose closed.

"Look, the nest is lined with black fur," Jeremy said, pointing to the nest. "Cool!"

"There's some white fur too," Angela said. "It may be a skunk's nest. We'd better get what we can carry and get out of here before they come back."

The four friends didn't always agree on things, but they certainly agreed on this, and continued salvaging what they could.

"Watch out for the skunks while we finish loading the wagon," Angela said.

"Maybe they don't live here anymore," said Jeannie.

"Well, I don't want to find out," said Jay. "Work faster!"

Every few minutes, one of them stopped to look around and make sure the skunks were nowhere in sight. Then, just as they finished loading the wagon, Jeannie scrunched her nose and said, "What is that smell?"

Everyone smelled the air like a pack of bloodhounds.

"We don't smell anything," the others said.

"Aaah – you're just smelling things, scaredy-cat!" said Jeremy.

"I'm sorry! I thought I smelled skunk," Jeannie said. "I guess it must have been you I smelled!" She stuck her tongue out at her brother.

"Ha-ha. Very funny." Jeremy returned the gesture.

The kids were tired and getting a little grumpy, especially the siblings.

"Awe, c'mon you guys. You can argue later. Let's get going," Angela said.

"You're right. I'm sorry, Jeremy," Jeannie said.

"Yeah, me too," Jeremy replied. "Let's go home."

CHAPTER 5

Rustling in the Woods

Angela grunted as she started pulling the heaping wagon toward home. Jay walked behind the wagon to help push and steady the load. Jeannie and Jeremy each grabbed one end of the stack of boards that were too long for the wagon and followed behind.

"Don't forget to keep an eye out for the skunks!" Angela said.

Jay said, "Uh, I think we'll *smell 'em* before we *see 'em*."

"Let me rephrase that," she said. "Keep a *nose* out for the skunks."

Everyone chuckled and hurried down the trail. Angela wanted to avoid a possible run-in with the skunks, so she pulled the wagon as fast as she could without tipping the load. Then – *Bump* – *Bump* – the two left wheels, first one, then the other, ran into a rut in the path.

"Whoa! Take it easy!" Jay said. He threw his arms around the wobbly stack of boards. "You almost dumped the load!"

"Sorry! I'll slow down and be more careful," Angela said. "I just don't wanna be here when those stinkers come home – and I really don't wanna get sprayed!"

"C'mon, let's go you guys!" Jeannie yelled from the back.

"Yeah, Let's go. These boards are heavy!" Jeremy said.

"Okay. Let's get going," Angela said. Then she shouted loud like a railroad conductor, "A-a-all abo-o-o-ard! This train is leaving the station!" Angela realized the pun she'd made. "Get it? All a-*board?*"

Jeremy wasn't in the mood for her jokes. "You and your puns!" he said in a mopey tone, "That was so funny I forgot to laugh."

"Don't you mean… It was so *punny* you forgot to laugh?" Jay cracked himself up, along with the others. Then, speaking fast, Jay said, "I thought it was *punny*. How about you, Jeannie? Did you think it was *punny*? Angela and I thought it was *punny*." I think Jeremy thought it was *punny*. He just doesn't want to admit it."

Jeremy sighed. "Ha – ha. Now let's get going!"

The others were enjoying Jays humor.

Then Jeannie said, "It was rather *punny*, Jeremy. Oops! I mean, funny." She giggled. "Oh, let's go home. You're just tired."

Jay chuckled, and yelled, "The *boards* are...all a-*board*. Let's get this train movin'! CHUGA-chuga-chuga-chuga, CHUGA-chuga-chuga-chuga, WOO-oo-WOO!" The fearless friends grinned and stomped their feet to Jay's chuga-chuga-woo-woos. Then they all sang out, "CHUGA-chuga-chuga-chuga, CHUGA-chuga-chuga-chuga, WOO-oo-WOO! Angela thrust her fist up and down with each WOO-oo-WOO, like an engineer blowing the train's steam whistle.

The gang's chatter grew quieter and their breathing louder as they wrestled the weight of their loads. They were about halfway home when suddenly they heard a rustling sound coming from the woods. The train came to an abrupt stop.

"What was that?" Jeannie said. She quickly turned her head and shifted her eyes toward the sound.

The kids strained to listen, as if their ears were high-powered radar listening devices. They looked in the direction of the sound, scanning the woods around them for any movement. Then it was quiet again.

Angela said in a soft voice, "Well, whatever it was, I don't hear it now. Let's keep going in case whatever it was is still out there."

The others nodded and moved slowly ahead, looking in all directions. About a dozen steps later, Jeannie said, "You guys... something's out there."

The tone in Jeannie's voice stopped the train to a dead halt, as if someone pulled the train's Emergency Stop cord.

"I don't hear anything," said Jay.

Jeannie put her finger to her lips, "Shh." Then she whispered, "I'm telling you, something's out there. Listen!"

This time they all heard the rustling sound, and it sounded closer than before. The brother-sister duo slowly eased their load down to the ground in case they had to make a run for it.

Angela's voice and finger trembled as she pointed to her left. "I just saw those bushes over there move."

"We did too!" Jeannie said. "Let's get out of here!" She and Jeremy picked up their stack of boards. "Go, go, go, you guys!"

Suddenly, a large animal with thick reddish-brown hair, big teeth, and a long, thick tail thundered out of the woods in front of Angela and stopped in the middle of the trail between the kids and home. Startled, everyone shouted and stopped dead in their tracks. Jeannie and Jeremy dropped their stack of boards. The creature lowered its head and shoulders, then fixed its gaze on the kids like a bull getting ready to charge. Did anyone hear their fearful shouts?

CHAPTER 6

Don't Turn Around!

"CASEY!" Everyone exhaled a giant sigh of relief.

Angela's dog was so happy to see her and her friends that he went on a hyper-run. Casey ran in a clockwise circle to the right around Angela and hurdled the loaded wagon with ease. Then he reversed his course, running counterclockwise to the left around the kids. His huge paws threw dirt into the air as he wheeled back around. Still a puppy, and a large one at that, Casey was clumsy and without full control of his brakes. He ran full steam ahead and jumped up on Angela, knocking her down. She laughed and wrapped her arms around him.

"You crazy dog! You scared us!" Angela said through his sloppy kisses. "How did you get loose?" Angie pushed Casey off, climbed to her feet, and took hold of the wagon handle once again. "Let's get going before anything else happens," she told the others. Angela patted the side of her leg and called out to the large out-of-control puppy, "C'mon Casey. Let's go home."

Everyone was glad it was Casey who had alarmed them and not the skunks. Once again, the brother-sister team lifted their long load. Jay took his position behind the wagon, and the train resumed its progress toward home, this time with Casey as their mascot.

Casey walked alongside Angela, taking an occasional detour into the woods. Once he returned with a stick in his mouth to play with. Tired from pulling the heavy load, Angela now walked backwards, pulling the wagon with both hands. The kids were making good progress when Jeannie wrinkled her nose again.

"I smell something," she said.

Jeremy rolled his eyes and groaned, "Not again."

"I do. I smell skunk!" Jeannie said.

Jeannie and Jeremy knew what skunks smelled like because a skunk had once gotten into their basement through the firewood chute. So, once again, the kids stuck their noses in the air and inhaled. Sure enough, they each drew in a snoot-full of stinky air.

"Jeannie's right – that's skunk." Jeremy said.

"I told you so!" Before Jeannie could say another word, she froze as stiff as the boards they were carrying. "Angela! Stop!" she said. "Don't turn around."

Of course, Angela's first impulse was to turn around. She hesitated, but her curiosity got the best of her and she turned around to see why she shouldn't turn around. Angela stopped, raised her eyebrows and widened her eyes; the wagon handle fell to the ground with a clunk. Angela wasn't just petrified – she was skunk-ified! A mama skunk and her three babies had just waddled onto the trail about twenty feet ahead of her.

Jeannie said through clenched teeth. "Angela! I told you – *don't* turn around! "Nobody move."

Angela was scared speechless – which rarely happened.

The boys each took one wide step to the side and leaned out just enough to see what the problem was.

Jay was yelling on the inside, but he whispered on the outside, "Skunks! I think we should run!"

"No!" Jeremy whispered. "My dad said to never run. He said they will only spray if they feel threatened."

"What else did your dad say?" Jay asked.

"My dad said they can only shoot their stink about ten feet, so we should be okay. They'll get Angela before us." Jeremy said.

Scared out of her stupor, Angela said, "Thanks a lot, Jeremy!"

Suddenly they heard rustling in the woods again!

Jay slapped his hands on his head and yell-whispered, "Casey's gonna scare the skunks!" Then he said to Jeremy, "If the mama skunk sprays Casey or Angela, maybe she won't have anything left to spray us with."

Jeremy quickly responded, "No, it doesn't work that way. My dad told me they can spray five or six times before running out. That means... she has enough stink spray for all of us!"

Angela's heart thudded inside her chest. She shook her head slowly and whispered, "Oh, man, Casey's gonna get sprayed." Concerned, Angela looked at Jay and said, "We're all gonna get sprayed."

CHAPTER 7

High-Tailing It Home

Angela's big brother, Brian, had just arrived home from working at his summer job. Sarah and Matt ran to welcome him home.

"Hi, you guys!" Brian squatted down to catch Sarah as she flew into his open arms for a big hug. Matty wasn't missing out on the fun. He jumped on his big brother's back while he was stooped low.

"Hi, Mom. I'm home," Brian said. The heavenly aroma of freshly baked cookies filled his nostrils. "Something sure smells good." He followed his nose to the kitchen with the two kids in tow; Sarah sitting on his right foot with her legs and arms clamped tightly around his leg; and Matt riding piggy-back with a choke hold around his neck.

"You're walking funny today," his mom said, keeping a straight face and pretending to not see the little kids. "What's wrong with your back and your leg?"

Brian joined in on the *Where are the kids?* game with his mom.

"Yeah. I'm having a hard time standing up straight. My leg feels extremely heavy and stiff, and I'm having a hard time breathing."

"Hey, it's us!" Sarah said.

"Yeah, it's us!" Matty echoed.

Brian and their mom pretended they didn't hear them.

"Where are the kids?" she asked Brian.

"I don't know. They must be playing upstairs or hiding."

"We're right here!" Sarah said louder than before.

"I don't see them. Do you?" their mom said.

Brian and his mom looked all around them, except at where the kids were.

"That's weird," he said. "I can hear them - but I can't see them."

Sarah jumped up, waved her arms, and said, "We're right here!"

"Well, there you are!" Brian said. "We couldn't find you."

Everyone laughed. That game never got old.

"It's so quiet in here," Brian said. He took a big bite of warm cookie. "Where's Angie?"

"She and her friends are in the woods on a treasure hunt."

"What do you mean… treasure hunt?"

"They're salvaging boards from a heap she found in the woods for us to use when we build her treehouse."

"So she's finally getting a treehouse. She's been begging for one, well, like, forever. Maybe that'll finally shut her up about it."

"Oh. She is beyond excited. Why don't you surprise them and see if they need any help?"

"Okay. Just point me in their direction." Brian grabbed two more cookies to eat on the way.

They stepped onto the porch and she pointed across the cul-de-sac to the trail. Just then, Brian realized that Casey was missing.

"Hey, where's Casey?" he asked. "Did Angie and the gang take him with them?"

"No. He must have gotten loose and went to find her," she said. "Take his leash with you just in case you need it."

Brian grabbed Casey's leash off the hook just inside the door. He cleared the back steps in two long strides, jogged across the cul-de-sac, and started down the trail. Brian was a good big brother - fun, smart, caring, and adventure-loving like Angela. He was also a bit of a daredevil – always willing to try something new. Brian loved his sister, and was protective of her, but he also loved teasing and pulling jokes on her. So it wasn't unusual as Brian walked along the trail to be plotting a way to sneak up on Angie and her friends.

Meanwhile, further down the trail, Angela couldn't see Casey, but she could hear him getting closer. She called out to Casey, hoping she could get a hold of his collar before he saw the skunks.

"Casey! Come here, Casey!" Angela saw the bushes moving, and then out popped Casey. She slapped her thighs and called to him in a playful voice. "Come on, boy!" she said, urging him to come to her. "Good boy! Come here!" Casey was nearly within reach, but it was too late. His attention was quickly diverted from Angela when he spotted – and smelled – the skunks. Casey's presence alarmed the mama skunk who quickly raised her tail toward him as a warning. Casey barked a warning back to her and her babies, as if to say, *Hey, you stinkers! You stay away from my sister and her friends!*

The cute baby skunks, called kits, were too young to shoot their musky spray, but that didn't keep them from smelling like they could. The babies mimicked their mama's action by snapping their tails straight up in the air – first one, then two, then three, just as if they knew what they were doing.

Having never seen skunks before, Casey somehow knew to keep his distance from them. He barked continually, bouncing left and right halfway between the skunks and Angela. Casey was unaware of what could happen if he scared the mama into defending herself and her family. Angela's persistent calls to him fell on deaf ears; he was too distracted by the black and white striped critters to heed her calls. The mama skunk turned toward Casey wherever he went. She was ready to fire if he got too close for comfort.

Brian hadn't gone far before he heard the kids yelling from further down the trail. "That sounds like trouble!" he said to himself. Sensing their need for help, Brian ran toward their shouts.

"Angie, where are you?" he yelled, but no reply. He shouted again so they would know that help was on the way. "Angela! Where are you?"

"Brian, we're over here! You need to get Casey before he gets sprayed by the skunks!"

"I'm coming!" he replied. Then Brian yelled, "Casey! Come here! Casey! Come on, boy!" Brian hoped the pup would obey his call, but so far he hadn't come.

Brian came around the last curve and beheld the situation. Casey was holding off the skunks, at least for now. Brian thought fast to come up with a plan. *Casey shouldn't see me if I go around through the trees to get behind him,* he thought. *I don't want to get sprayed, but I don't want Casey to get sprayed either. Oh boy, if I'm not careful, we'll both be taking a bath in tomato juice and sleeping outside tonight.*

Brian took a deep breath and thought, *Timing is everything! I only get one chance at this.* So he made a wide circle through the trees and underbrush until he was about ten feet behind Casey.

Unfortunately, the kids were so glad to see Brian that they stopped yelling and watched him instead. Now it was too quiet! Brian needed a distraction, and quick! He used hand signals to get the kids shouting to Casey again. When their yelling resumed, Brian moved slowly toward the dog. It was working. Casey was completely unaware of him.

The loud sound of Casey barking covered the crunching sound of the leaves and twigs under Brian's feet when he walked. He carefully timed his steps to Casey's barking; if Casey stopped, Brian stopped; if Casey barked, Brian walked.

Now, just one arm's length from completing his mission, Brian stopped. *Please don't let me get sprayed,* he prayed silently as he prepared to retrieve the retriever. Brian knew he had to lunge for Casey at just the right moment if he wanted to catch him on the first try. Brian knew that if he missed, not even his kung fu training could protect him from the skunks' pungent spray!

"I can't watch!" Jeannie said, covering her eyes with her hands. "I just know they're gonna get sprayed. Tell me when it's over."

Brian counted slowly under his breath, One...Two...Three! He lunged forward and grabbed for Casey's collar.

"Did he get him? Did they get sprayed?" Jeannie said, spreading her fingers just enough to peer between them at Angela.

Angela said, "I don't know, I closed my eyes too."

"I got Casey!" Brian yelled after snapping the leash onto Casey's collar. The surprise of seeing Brian was but a short-lived distraction from the skunks. After a quick hello, Casey resumed his barking. He barked and coughed as he strained against the leash toward the skunks. Brian pulled Casey backwards until they were an unintimidating distance from the skunks. Then he instructed the others in a calm, firm voice. "Everyone be quiet and slowly back up about 10 to 15 feet. I'm taking Casey home so he, and the skunks, will settle down. Then I'll come back for you. The skunks should leave once we back-off and give them some space."

The kids quieted down and slowly retreated, while Brian coaxed and pulled Casey until they were well out of sight of the skunks. Brian tried everything to urge Casey toward home. "C'mon, Casey. Let's go home! Do you want a treat? Dad's home!"

Finally, Casey ran freely alongside him as they got closer to home. Brian could barely keep up with his long strides, especially when they reached the cul-de-sac. Casey was tired and thirsty, so he headed straight to his water bowl and lapped non-stop until it was empty. Brian hooked the long chain attached to the doghouse onto Casey's collar so he couldn't follow him back into the woods. Exhausted, Casey stretched out on his belly in the cool grass to rest. Brian leaped up the steps and returned the leash to its hook inside the back door.

"Mom, I brought Casey home!" Brian hollered. "I'm going back to help the kids."

"Okay. I'll have a snack ready by the time you all get back."

Brian didn't tell his mom about the skunks because he didn't want her to worry. He was certain the kids were okay and they would all laugh about it later.

It turned out that the skunks did just as Brian said they would. When the mama skunk felt safe, she and her cute trio of kits lowered their tails and waddled into the woods.

"Aww, those baby skunks were so cute;" Angela said, "stinky, but cute. I'd have a skunk as a pet if they didn't stink."

"You're crazy!" Jay said. "You think all baby animals are cute."

"I know, but you have to admit, they really were cute," she said.

"Yeah, and if they didn't carry rabies!" Jeremy said.

"Oh, Jeremy! Don't be such a killjoy," Jeannie said. "They were cute, and I love how they waddle and follow each other in a line."

Jeremy shook his head and grumbled, "Girls!"

"C'mon." said Jay. "Let's get outta here before they come back."

"Okay, let's go," Angela said.

The fearless foursome didn't wait for Brian; like the skunks, they hightailed it out of there. Jeremy and Jeannie picked up their stack of long boards, Angela and Jay returned to their loaded wagon, and the weary foursome took off like a runaway train with no brakes, moving as fast as they could without running off the tracks and dumping their loads.

The kids made several trips that day; laughing and talking when they entered the woods; dragging their feet and panting when they exited. But this time, they came out of the woods running full-steam ahead and out of breath. Clearly, the 'Fearless Foursome' wasn't so fearless when it came to skunks.

Brian was surprised to see them emerging from the woods just as he was going back for them. They were a fast-moving train that wasn't stopping for anything, so Brian stepped aside to let them fly by. He said, "Hey, I was gonna…"

"Can't… talk now…. We're almost… there!" Angela panted.

Brian laughed as he watched them running toward the house. "You know you can slow down now!" he said. "There aren't any skunks around here!" He paused. "I'll tell Mom you're home!"

Jeannie and Jeremy dropped their load by the lumber pile while Angie and Jay parked the fully-loaded wagon along the other side of the pile. Then the tired kids flopped on the ground and lay on their backs huffing and puffing from their long run home. It wasn't long before one began to laugh, then another, and another, until they were laughing so hard their bellies jiggled like bowls of jelly.

The kids had completed their mission. No one got hurt, and no one got sprayed. It was a good day!

Then Jay noticed someone standing near him and lifted his head to see who it was. "Kelly! Hey, look. It's Kelly!" Jay said.

Still on their backs, the others popped their heads up in surprise. Then they propped themselves up on their elbows. "Kelly, you came!" the others resounded.

"Yeah, I just thought I'd take a break from my game to see how you guys were coming along with your project," Kelly said.

Angela pointed to the pile of boards, saying, "See for yourself."

The sweaty, dirty, exhausted friends rose to their feet, placed their hands on their hips, and gleamed with pride at the heap of lumber as if it was a mountain of gold.

Kelly's eyes widened. "Wow. That's quite a haul," he said.

"Yeah, and that's only part of the story," Angela said. "Wait till you hear how Casey almost got sprayed by skunks!"

Just then, Angela's mom stuck her head out the door and called, "Hey, kids! Come get some chocolate chip cookies... still warm... right out of the oven!"

After all their hard work, the famished foursome couldn't wait to sink their teeth into the yummy, ooey gooey cookies. Their feet sounded like thunder as they raced up the steps to the house.

Kelly hung his head and turned to go home. "I'll see you guys later," he whined.

Angela looked at Kelly, shrugged her shoulders, and said, "Hey! Where are you going? Come in and have some cookies so we can tell you about the skunks."

Surprised by Angela's invitation, Kelly spun around and said, "Really? Are you sure?"

"Yeah. C'mon," she said, waving him inside.

The air in the kitchen was heavy with the smell of chocolate and butter. Jay tilted his head back and sucked in the sweet aroma. The others did the same.

"These cookies smell so good!" Jay said, reaching for a cookie.

He raised the cookie under his nose, smelled it, and took a big bite. "Mmmm," he said. "This sure beats the smell of skunks."

"Mm-hmm," the others mumbled through chocolatey lips.

Angela hugged her mom around her waist. "Thank you, Mom."

"Thank you, Mrs. M!" the other kids said.

"I sure am glad you guys came to see me the other day," Kelly mumbled through a mouthful of cookie.

Each of the kids, armed with a handful of cookies and a glass of cold milk, went outside and took a seat against one of the tall oaks around the woodpile to enjoy their treat. They ate slowly to enjoy every bite. Homemade cookies never smelled or tasted better than they did that day; perfectly crisp on the outside; chewy on the inside; and loaded with morsels of molten chocolatey goodness. The kids laughed as they told Kelly about their skunk stand-off. The story grew bigger as each one told their part of the story.

"That sounds exciting, and a little scary too," Kelly said. "I don't know if I'm sad or glad that I missed out on the adventure."

Either way, Kelly was happy to be with his friends again. He hadn't laughed like that in a long time. The kids continued talking in the shade of the oaks. They discussed the fun things they might do together from Angela's Adventure List, which included playing in Angela's new treehouse. Then they all headed home to shower and rest after the long, unforgettable day. They couldn't wait to tell their parents the tale of the skunk stand-off, and how Brian had swooped in to rescue them.

Angela showered and dressed. Then she flopped across her bed. A smile crossed her face and she closed her eyes. "This bed feels so good," she said in a whisper. "I'll lie here for just a few..."

More than an hour later her mom called out, "Angela! Come down for supper!" Nothing. "Angie!" Nothing again. Then her mom shouted even louder, "Angela! Come down for supper!"

Groggy from her sleep, Angela answered, "Yeah?" She looked at her clock, but she was so sleepy she didn't know if it was 6:30 in the morning or 6:30 in the evening.

"Okay, I'm coming," Angela mumbled.

Normally Angela helped her mom by setting the table for supper with a plate, silverware, napkin, and glass at each place, but today her mom let her off the hook because of her hard day.

Angela heard a car door close. That woke her up! She ran to the window. "Dad's home!" She flung the door open for him.

"Hi, Dad." He grunted when Angela hugged him tight. Seeing the brown paper bag from the hardware store in his hand, she asked, "What's in the bag?"

Her dad left his shoes by the door and loosened his tie. "You'll find out after supper."

"I hate being kept in suspense."

Her dad grinned and gave her a sly wink. "That's why I do it."

Angela crossed her arms and pretended to frown.

"What have you and your friends been up to today?" he asked.

"You won't believe the day we had! We hauled a million boards from the woods; Mom made us a picnic lunch; Casey got loose and came to find us; we kids and Casey almost got sprayed by cute, smelly skunks; Brian saved us; and Mom made us the very best chocolate chip cookies ever!"

"Well, it sounds like you had quite the day. Why don't you tell me about it during supper. I can't wait to hear about the cute smelly skunks." Then he waved his nose through the air from left to right, taking in a big whiff. "Speaking of smelly… it smells so good in here I could eat the air!"

"Me too." Then Angela pretended to take a big chomp of air. "Mmm… so good," she said.

Then her dad took a big bite of air. "It tastes as good as it smells."

"Time for dinner!" Angela's mom called from the kitchen.

Her dad patted his small, round belly and said to Angela, "I don't know about you, but I don't think I could eat another bite."

Angela stuck out her tummy, so it looked like her dad's, and patted it. "Me either. I'm stuffed."

Her dad smiled and placed the brown bag from the hardware store in one arm, then he put his other arm around Angela's shoulders. Angela smiled back at her dad, then put her arm around his waist, and the two sauntered to the dinner table.

"I sure hope you two are hungry," Angela's mom said. "The kids and I made you a nice supper."

Angela's dad grinned and winked at Angie. Then, placing his hands on his tummy, he said, "We couldn't eat another bite."

CHAPTER 8

What's in the Bag?

Angela's mom was a wonderful cook and baker; so good that her mom rarely had to call more than once to get the family to the dinner table. Tonight, she made Angela's favorite meal – simple, yet delicious – a reward for Angie's determination and hard work.

The lip-smacking aroma wafting through the air enticed the family to the table. Angela's dad took his seat at the head of the table and set the hardware store bag on the floor beside him. Angela plopped onto the chair next to him.

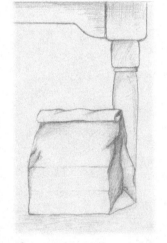

"My favorites!" she said. "Goulash, garlic bread, salad, and chocolate cake! Well, maybe not the salad… but everything else." Her eyes danced and her stomach turned cartwheels at the sight. Angela loved bread. She could make a meal of garlic bread and nothing else! But as far as she was concerned, the only good things about salad were the ranch-style dressing and croutons (toasted *bread* cubes). She spooned a large helping of goulash onto her plate, tucked two pieces of soft, buttery garlic bread alongside it. Then she filled the remaining space on her plate with a small amount of salad and topped it with plenty of ranch-style dressing and croutons. Angela looked at her plate of food and said, "Thanks, Mom."

"You're welcome. You earned it. I'm proud of you for how hard you worked today. You didn't give up, and you kids stuck together even when the skunks scared you."

"Thanks. That means a lot, but… can we eat now? I'm starving!"

"We can eat after we pray for the meal," her dad said.

Angela shot her hand into the air. "I'll pray!" Without delay, she folded her hands, bowed her head, and closed her eyes. "Dear God, thank you for this food. Amen."

Then Angela stuffed her mouth with a huge fork-full of goulash, followed by a big bite of garlic bread. "Mmm," she said.

Her dad chuckled. "Well, that prayer was short and sweet."

Angela nodded. "Mmm-hmm." Her mouth was too full to talk.

"You must really want that treehouse if you're willing to work that hard for it."

Angela swallowed her food with a gulp and said, "I sure do!"

"I'm pleased at how well you four kids get along," her mom said. "It was sure nice seeing Kelly here today. It's been a while."

"Mmm-hmm," Angela nodded and gobbled down her meal in record time, finishing before everyone else. She glanced at the paper bag on the floor and secretly agonized over what was in it.

"Did you even taste your food?" her dad said.

Angela gave him one contented nod, then rested her chin on her hands to wait for everyone else to finish eating.

"Tell your dad about your day while I get the cake," her mom said. "I'm sure it was *much* more exciting than his was."

Angela told him about her exciting day. Her dad reared back and laughed when she got to the part about the skunks.

"I have a skunk story too," he said. "Would you like to hear it?"

"Sure, I would!" Angie said.

"Well, it goes like this...

The skunk sat on a stump.
The stump thunk the skunk stunk,
And the skunk thunk the stump stunk.
Which one stunk, the skunk or the stump?"

"Hey! That's a tongue twister, not a story!" Angie said.

"Yes, and it's even better when you can say it really fast. Give it a try while I finish eating."

Angela practiced the skunk tongue twister so she could tell it to her friends, without stinking at it. Her dad was eating at a snail's pace, listening to her, and enjoying every bite. She wished he would hurry and eat as fast as she did. Everyone listened and giggled as Angie tripped over her twisted tongue time after time. Finally, she looked at her dad and said, "I think I've got it! What do you think?"

Her dad said slowly, "I *thunk* you did so well that you'll *stump* your friends without *stunking* like a *skunk*." He grinned at her and took another bite of his supper.

Angela laughed; her mom smiled big and shook her head; Sarah and Matty laughed along – even though they were too young to understand his corny humor.

"I also know a song about skunks. Would you like to hear it?" her dad said.

"Yeah!" the three kids hollered.

Their mom smiled and said, "Remember – you asked for it."

Their dad sat up tall in his chair and cleared his throat loudly in preparation to sing. "Listen carefully, it goes to the tune of *A Turkey in the Straw*," her dad said, then he sang loud.

> *Oh, I stuck my head*
> *In the little skunk's hole*
> *And the little skunk said,*
> *"Well, bless my soul!*
> *Take it out! Take it out!*
> *Take it out! Take it out! Remove it!"*
>
> *Oh, I didn't take it out*
> *So the little skunk said*
> *"If you don't take it out,*
> *You'll wish you were dead,*
> *Take it out! Take it out!*
> *Take it out! Take it out! Remove it!"*
> *PSSSSST! I removed it too late!"*

Angela and little kids smiled as he sang the funny little ditty.

"Hey, we could have used that song today!" Angela said. Then she sang out loud, "PSSSSST! I *almost* removed it too late!"

Everyone shared a good laugh. Then Angela propped one elbow on the table, rested her chin in her hand and fixed her gaze on her dad. He winked a sly wink to his wife who was seated at the other end of the table that said, *watch this*.

With just one last bite of cake remaining, her dad loaded his fork, raised it in line with his mouth, and stared at the chocolatey bite of heaven. The family watched his funny antics. Then, like feeding a toddler, he flew the food-laden fork through the air in two large circles and plunged the tasty bite into his wide-open mouth. Then he swept the empty fork from between his clenched lips and held it high. "Mmm," he said as he slowly chewed and savored the bite.

Everyone laughed except Angela. She slapped her hand on her forehead and said, "Aw, c'mon! Could you eat any slower?"

Her dad laughed so hard his belly shook. Angela couldn't help but laugh along.

Then her dad slapped his hands together and said in an energetic voice, "Who knows what tomorrow is?"

Angela raised both hands and said, "It's TREEHOUSE DAY."

Like Angela, Sarah and Matty echoed, "Treehouse Day!"

Then Angela's mom said, "You and Angie go to the garage and get things organized for tomorrow so we can get an early start."

"Okay. Let's get going, Angie," her dad said.

"Wait a minute." Angie pointed to the bag. "What's in the bag?"
Her dad smiled and pushed the bag toward her with his foot.
"See for yourself."

Angela picked up the bag, set it on her lap and peeked inside.

"Wha'd you get?" Sarah said.

"Yeah, wha'd you get?" Matty said.

Angela reached into the bag and pulled out a zippered canvas
bag and set it on the table in front of her. "Hmm," she said, "it looks
like… a tool bag."

"Look inside," her dad said.

Angela opened the zipper. A puzzled look crossed her face.
"Tools," she said. "Gee, thanks – I think."

"They're not *just* tools. They're your very own tools. I thought
you could use them when we build your treehouse." Then he said,
"And… maybe, since you have your own tools now, you won't
leave mine out in the rain."

Angela tucked her chin and said, "Sorry, Dad."

"Well?" her mom asked. "What's in the bag?"

Angela perked up. "Let me see." She looked into the bag. "I got
a hammer, and it's just my size." She held it up for everyone to see.

"I want a hammuw," said Matty.

"You'll get a hammer when you're a little older," his dad said.

One-at-a-time, Angela held the tools up for everyone to see, then
placed them on the table. "I got eye protection glasses, work gloves,
two screwdrivers – a flat one and an 'X' one, a folding saw, and a

tape measure. Thanks, Dad. You're right," she said, returning the tools to the bag, "I can use these when we build the treehouse, and when I decorate it."

"Get going, you two," Her mom said. "Have fun in the garage while I clean up and get the little ones bathed and into bed."

Angela and her dad pushed away from the table. Angela led the way, walking with a little skip in her step.

"C'mon, Dad. Let's go see what we can find for the treehouse."

Her dad smiled at her enthusiasm. "You sure are peppy after the long day you had."

"Not really. I'm kinda wiped out, and believe it or not, I can't wait to go to bed."

Her dad chuckled. "You must be tired if you're excited about going to bed early."

"I am. But I'm more excited about the treehouse than I am about sleeping," Angela said. "The treehouse wins – hands down."

"We'd better hurry up then so you can get some sleep and recharge your batteries for tomorrow."

They gathered screws and nails, sawhorses, extension cords for the power tools, regular tools, and any other items that might be useful. They also found two bundles of shingles that were left over from building their house to use on the roof. They neatly stacked everything near the door for the next morning.

"That's a good start. We'll buy anything else we need from the lumberyard tomorrow," her dad said.

This was one time Angela didn't mind going to bed. She washed her face and hands, brushed her teeth, slipped into her pajamas, and crawled into her cozy bed. She was as eager for sleep as she was for her treehouse. Angela grabbed the covers and pulled them up under her chin. Then she flutter-kicked her feet like a swimmer and squealed to herself, "I can't wait for tomorrow!" For a moment, her excitement outweighed her exhaustion, and she sang softly, "I'm getting a treehouse – I'm getting a treehouse." Then Angela smiled, flipped onto her belly, and punched her feather pillow a few times. She scrunched her pillow into just the right shape, wrapped her arms around it, laid down her weary head, and fell fast asleep with a smile on her face and a treehouse in her dreams.

CHAPTER 9

Construction Begins

Angela's eyes cracked open a little earlier than usual. She must have been tired since she awoke in the same position she had fallen asleep in. She rolled onto her back and let out a long squeak as she stretched from head to toe. Then something strange interrupted her much-needed stretch. When Angela inhaled deeply through her nose, the corners of her mouth drew up and her shoulders rose toward her ears. When she exhaled, everything fell back into place. It happened again! *What is this strange happening?* she wondered.

Angela soon discovered the cause… Bacon! A wonderful, smoky aroma of bacon cooking filled Angela's bedroom from the kitchen below. She sat up straight in her bed and closed her eyes. Again, her shoulders rose in sync with the corners of her mouth as she breathed in another long whiff of the bacon-filled air. "Mmm… bacon." Angela's eyes popped open wide. "The treehouse!" she said aloud. Angela jumped out of bed, dressed quickly and ran down the stairs to the awaiting breakfast.

"Thanks, Mom! I could smell the bacon in my bedroom," Angela said. She put several strips of bacon on her plate, along with some eggs and toast.

"I knew that would get you out of bed," her mom said.

"You can wake me up like that anytime!"

Angela swallowed the last big swig of her orange juice. "Let's hurry and finish so we can get started on the treehouse."

"Sorry. I can't help today," Brian said. "I have to work all day."

Disappointed, Angela said, "That's okay."

"I'm sorry too," her dad said. "I just got called into work, so we won't be able to work on the treehouse today after all. Maybe next weekend."

Angela's shoulders slumped, she hung her head and whined, "Okay. I understand."

Her dad leaned back in his chair and rubbed his full belly. Then he forced it out to the size of a basketball and gave it a few hard pats. Everyone laughed, except Angela.

"Really?" she said, clearly upset about the treehouse delay.

Her dad placed his elbows on the table and clasped his hands.

"No…not really!" he said. Then he hopped up from his chair and said with great enthusiasm, "Let's go build a treehouse!"

"Ooooh! I can't believe you did that to me!" Angela said. Then she jumped onto his back and growled, pretending to attack him.

He spun around a couple times and snarled back at her. The little kids laughed at their silly antics.

Angela's mom laughed, but then said, "Hey! No monkeying around inside! Take it outside and start looking around for a good treehouse spot while I clean up the breakfast dishes."

Angela whispered something to her dad, then slid down his back. They nodded to each other and went into the kitchen.

"We're going to help so you can go outside *with* us," Angela's dad said. "I'll wash!" he said loud.

"I'll dry!" said Angela.

"Well – I guess I'll put away," her mom said.

Angela disliked doing dishes, but this time she was happy to help if it meant getting to work on the treehouse sooner. Chitter-chatter about the treehouse filled the kitchen as they worked together as a team. Her dad washed and rinsed, then handed off to Angela. Angela dried and handed off to her mom. Sarah put the silverware in the drawer, while Matty played with a toy truck under the kitchen table. Their assembly line ran like a well-oiled machine and the kitchen was clean in no time.

Angela's mom stepped between Angela and her dad and said, "Thank you for your help. It was very thoughtful, and – it was extra special because I didn't have to ask for it."

"You're welcome," Angela said. "It was almost fun doing it together... *almost*."

Her dad smiled and said, "Yes, it was.

"Group hug!" Angela's mom said.

The three put their arms around each other with their heads together and hugged. Sarah and Matty squeezed between their legs and got in on the hug too.

"Okay, now. Let's go outside and get busy!" said her mom.

Together, the family went outside to find the perfect treehouse location. Angela's mom carried a notepad, pencil, and a measuring tape; her dad carried Sarah on his shoulders; and Angela carried Matty on her back, piggy-back style.

Angela's dad pondered their options. "If we build it on the east side of the yard, it may be a little too close to the house. There are wild raspberries and poison ivy on the west side, and the south side is too close to the neighbors behind us."

Angela said, "So, the treehouse needs be far enough from the house to feel like we're in the woods, but close enough to the house for when we need to use the bathroom or we get scared... *not that we'll ever get scared.*"

Her parents looked at each other and exchanged a look that said, *She'll get scared – all kids do.*

Angela continued, "We also don't want to upset the neighbors behind us if we're too loud – because, we usually are."

Her dad smiled. "Yes, you usually are," he said.

Angela's mom said, "I agree. Besides that, it needs to be an easy walk for Sarah and Matty since they're little, because you know they'll want to play in the treehouse with you too."

"Yeah, we wanna play in it too," Sarah said.

"Me, too," Matty echoed.

With his right arm pointing south and his left arm pointing east, her dad said, "Let's spread out and search this section of the yard for the best trees. Yell out if you find a good spot."

Angela, with Matty and their mom walked one way; her dad and Sarah walked the other way. Everyone looked up and down, and all around, as they went. Some of the trees were too small; some were nice, but too close together, or too far apart.

Angela looked around, then asked Matty, "Where do you think we should build the treehouse?"

He shrugged his little shoulders, and said, "I dunno."

Sarah had a bird's-eye view from atop her daddy's shoulders. She pointed to some trees and said, "I like those big trees."

"Let's go check them out. Hold on tight," her dad said.

Sarah held tight to her daddy's neck as he waded through the thick underbrush.

"Good job, Sarah," he said. "I think this is the spot."

Sarah clapped her little hands together and patted the top of her dad's head. He yelled and waved to the others to come see the trees.

"Hey! I think we found the perfect grouping of trees over here!"

"Hold on, Matty!" Angela said. "Let's go see!" Angela held tight to Matt and trotted through the ferns toward her dad. Her mom followed at a fast pace.

"Yay-ay-ay-ay! Giddy u-u-up." Matty's voice bounced with Angela's strides.

Their dad pointed to the tall trees. "Well, what do you think? Sarah found them."

Angie tried to imagine what it would be like to have a treehouse between the cluster of tall trees.

"This spot is fairly close to Jeannie's house too," she said.

"And these trees make a nearly perfect rectangle," her dad said.

Angela's mom looked at the path leading to the house. "I think this location is ideal. It's not too far, but far enough to feel secluded. "What do you think, Angie?" her mom said.

"I love it! It's perfect. Thank you, Sarah!"

Angela's mom and dad took some measurements, then went inside to make plans, while the kids played outside. Their mom sketched a picture of what they thought the treehouse might look like. They decided to build it just a few feet off the ground, rather than high in the trees like most treehouses. That way the little kids could go in and out safely. Angela thought that was a good idea too. Their parents made a list of the additional supplies they needed so her dad could go to the lumberyard.

Sarah and Matt played on the back deck while Angela and her mom carried the tools and supplies to the treehouse building site. They had everything organized and ready to go when her dad returned with the remaining supplies.

"Let's get started!" he said.

Angie helped by sorting the salvaged lumber by length, while her parents marked the trees for where to put the frame for the treehouse floor.

Angela's mom learned her building skills by helping her father when she was growing up. Angela, in turn, was going to learn skills from her father *and* her mother.

Angela helped her dad by holding the end of a board steady while he sawed it to the needed length; she helped her mom by holding the boards while her mom nailed or screwed them into place. Sometimes Angela even got to pound nails in with her new hammer. She liked hammering the best!

Z-Z-Z-ZING. BAM, BAM, BAM, BAM, BAM. The sounds of construction were like music to Angela's ears – LOUD, but musical. It wasn't long before they were screwing the plywood flooring on top of the framework between the trees. Finally, her dad put the last screw into the flooring and sat back on his heels to rest.

"I'm ready for a lunch break," he said.

"Me too," said Angela.

"I'll go get lunch ready," her mom said.

On her way in, Angela's mom sent Sarah and Matty down the path to Angela and their dad. "Here come the little ones," she said.

Sarah was like a little mom to Matty; always looking out for her little brother. Angie and her dad smiled as they watched Sarah holding Matty's hand as they walked down the trail. Their dad trotted down the path and met them halfway. Then he scooped them up, one in each arm, and trotted back to the treehouse.

Angela climbed up and tromped around on the new treehouse floor to see how sturdy it was.

"We wanna do that too!" Sarah said.

"Me do dat too!" said Matt.

The three kids held hands and danced around on the new floor.

The kids' dance of celebration captured their mom's attention as she was setting the table for lunch. She was overjoyed by the kids' special bond.

After a satisfying lunch, Angela and her dad resumed their work on the treehouse, while her mom tucked the little ones into bed for their afternoon nap. Then her mom returned to the treehouse project and hung the baby monitor on a nail in a nearby tree so she could listen for the kids to wake up.

Refueled and ready to work, their next step was to build the tree-house walls. First, they built the two long side walls, and then the back-end wall. They added a small window to the long wall facing the house, and a larger window to the back-end wall. The treehouse was taking shape.

Before long the sound of two happy, well-rested children rang out from the tree-mounted baby monitor and Angela's mom hustled inside to get them. They were happy to see that the treehouse now had walls and windows.

"But there's no top," Sarah said. "What if it rains? Where's the door?"

"Yeah," Angela said. "What are we going to do for a door?"

"We've talked about that, but we're not sure yet," her mom said.

Then her dad said, "Let's wash up and go to the Panther Drive-in for an early supper so your mom doesn't have to cook. We'll discuss the door options while we eat, then build the roof and door when get back home."

The kids cheered. They loved going to the Panther drive-in that had the cool food trays that hooked onto the car windows. But today they would sit at a picnic table so their mom could sketch their ideas. Angela helped the little kids with their food while her parents ate and discussed door options. Then her dad had a clever idea for the treehouse door.

"I've got it!" he said. "What if the door is like a drawbridge?"

"What do you mean?" Angela asked.

"When it's closed, it'll be a wall," he said, "and when it's open, it'll be a ramp for going in and out of the treehouse."

"Cool! Nobody will have a treehouse like mine!" Angela said.

Angela's mom grabbed her pencil and made quick strokes on the paper of what she thought the drawbridge might look like.

"Everyone finish eating," their dad said. "We still have a lot of work to do."

Angie played with Sarah and Matty while her parents built the roof. Then they made the roof waterproof by topping it with roofing tar paper and shingles. Now just one thing remained – the drawbridge door.

"Can I spray the roof with water to see if it leaks?" Angela asked.

"That's a good idea," her mom said. "You get the hose ready while we take a short lemonade break. Make sure you keep it out of the way so we won't trip over it… and don't spray the roof until we're all finished with the door so we aren't walking in mud."

"Yes, ma'am! I'll get it!"

Angela ran to the house. She untangled and pulled the long, awkward hose through the yard until it was a safe distance from the work area.

The 'three peas in a pod' giggled and crawled around in the treehouse while their mom and dad worked on the door. Her parents anchored the door in place with three sturdy hinges on the bottom edge. Then they attached several strips of wood across the door for traction, so the kids wouldn't slip when going in and out of the treehouse. Of course, Angela had to try it out. She walked up and down the ramp a couple times. Sarah and Matty followed her up the ramp and into the treehouse.

"How am I going to close the drawbridge?" Angela asked.

Her dad smiled. "We have a plan."

The three kids watched from inside the treehouse as their parents' plan took shape.

First, they attached a long piece of rope to each top corner of the door. Second, they threaded the ropes through a hole above the doorway, and then tied the ropes together so they couldn't fall back through the hole. Third, her dad installed a hook on the inside to latch it shut. Last, her mom and dad installed sliding bolt latches on the outside of the door to hold it closed when not in use.

"There," her dad said, placing his hands on his hips. "That was the finishing touch. Let's give it a try."

Angela pulled on the ropes. The door was heavier than she expected, but Angela was determined to do it by herself for when she was in the treehouse alone. Angela pulled harder until the door raised into place, then she fastened it shut.

"It worked!" she said. "It was hard to pull, but I did it."

"It should get easier the more you use it," her mom said.

Then Angela unhooked the door and lowered it back down.

"Now can I spray the roof?

"Yes," her dad said. "Close the door and latch it shut, then go turn the water on."

Angela ran to the house and turned on the water spigot. Then she returned as fast as a rabbit and armed herself with the hose.

"Okay, hose it down!" her dad said.

Angela sprayed the water full force over the entire treehouse for several minutes. Then she lowered the drawbridge and crawled all around the inside of the treehouse to inspect it for leaks.

"It's dry!" she shouted.

"Great! Then I declare the treehouse FINISHED," her dad said.

It was shortly before dusk and the sunlight was quickly fading. Angela walked around her new digs, inspecting every square inch. Its rustic beauty was perfect in her eyes.

"Thank you for my treehouse, Mom and Dad. I love it!"

Angela's parents hugged her between them like an Angie sandwich.

"You are very welcome," her dad said.

"We had fun building it *for* you… and *with* you," said her mom.

Angela couldn't believe her eyes – she had a treehouse!

It had been a long, yet rewarding day; everyone was tired. Even the sun was turning in for the night, tucking the earth under its chin like a cozy blanket.

"Can I sleep in my treehouse tonight?" Angela asked her mom.

"Yes, you can. Will you be okay out here by yourself?"

Just then Angela realized she did indeed feel a little uneasy about staying alone in the treehouse for the first time.

"Can I ask Jeannie to stay with me?"

"Sure," her mom said. "It's getting late, so we'll put away the tools while you call Jeannie and get your stuff ready."

"Thank you!" Angela said while running to the house.

"Make sure it's alright with her parents!" her mom yelled.

A few minutes later, Angela poked her head out the door and hollered to her mom, "Jeannie's mom said yes!"

"Okay! Get what you need and bring it out. It's getting dark!"

Angela stuffed a can of bug repellent spray and a deck of playing cards into her pillowcase, plus granola bars, fruit, popcorn, and bottled water to share with Jeannie. She washed up, brushed her teeth, and slipped into her comfy pajamas. Angela tucked her sleeping bag under one arm, hugged her lumpy, loaded pillow in her other arm, then grabbed her flashlight and scampered down the stairs. She flicked on the outside light just as her parents were coming inside.

"I'm all set," Angela said, sliding her feet into her raggedy sneakers that were sitting by the door.

"We'll come check on you and say goodnight in a bit," her mom said as Angela hustled out the door and hopped down the steps.

A faint orange glow was all that remained of the day as the sun slipped below the horizon. Angela turned on her flashlight and skipped down the path toward the treehouse. She spotted Jeannie weaving in and out through the trees between their houses, shining her flashlight ahead of her. Jeannie was in polkadot pajamas with a plaid blanket draped around her shoulders like a shawl, a sleeping bag under her arm, and a fluffy flowered pillow in her hand.

"Here I come!" Jeannie said.

Angela held up her bulging pillow. "I have some chocolate chip granola bars, bananas, a bag of popcorn and two bottles of water."

"My mom sent crispy peanut butter and marshmallow cereal treats, pretzels and juice boxes," Jeannie said.

"We may get scared, but we won't get hungry," Angela said.

The girls laughed and made their way up the drawbridge.

"I can't believe I'm sleeping in my very own treehouse tonight," Angie said. "Pinch me, I think I'm dreaming."

Jeannie pinched Angie's arm.

"Ouch!" Angie rubbed her arm. "Why'd you do that?"

"You told me to."

"Yeah, but I didn't think you'd do it!"

The girls laughed again, and rolled out their sleeping bags side by side. Then they removed the goodies from their pillowcases, leaned their pillows against the back-end wall, and stood their flashlights beside them in case they got scared or had to go inside during the night. Angela switched on the small battery-powered lamp, and the Christmas lights hanging from the ceiling. Then the girls sat on their sleeping bags and played a couple games of cards and enjoyed their snacks.

The backyard was aglow with the firefly's on-again off-again light show as the sun settled beneath the western horizon. The air was filled with the deafening buzz of locusts, the high-pitched song of frogs in the nearby creek – their vocal sacs bulging, and the chattering of two happy girls in a treehouse. Angie turned off the lamp and the girls lay on their backs, their heads on their pillows, to watch the firefly ballet through the open doorway. Angela talked non-stop about the treehouse, and all the fun they would have in it.

All was going well until Jeannie heard... *Crack – Snap.* She sat up straight. "What was that?"

"Now, don't start that again. I didn't hear anything."

"You didn't hear it because you were too busy talking!"

Snap – Crunch – Crunch – Crunch – Silence.

"I heard that!" Angela whispered. She sat up straight. "Listen!"

The startled girls were scared speechless. They quietly scooted backward until their backs pressed against the back-end wall. They grabbed their flashlights and shined them out the open doorway.

Then they heard – *Crunch* – *Crunch* – *Snap* – *Crack* – *Crunch*, then *Silence* again.

Angela raised her eyebrows. "I heard that!" Her voice shook a little. "Some-*thing* or some-*one* is out there," Angela whispered.

"Should we scream for help?" Jeannie said.

BANG.

Something hit the outside of the back wall between them. The girls screamed and scrambled to the middle of their sleeping bags to get away from the big window. Jeannie shined her flashlight at the window while Angie shined her flashlight out the door. They hoped the light would scare away whatever was out there.

"Mua-ha-ha-ha-ha-ha-ha." A creepy laugh came from outside the treehouse. A face suddenly appeared in the window!

The frightened girls screamed again and quickly focused both flashlights on the terrifying face pressed against the screen.

"BRIAN." Both girls shouted and scowled at him.

"I didn't scare you, did I?" Brian said laughing.

"No! We knew it was you." Angela said, acting tough.

"Yeah, right. That's why you screamed so loud – and not just once, but twice," he said, laughing.

"Well, maybe just a little," Angie said.

Just then, two faces appeared in the treehouse doorway.

"Ready for bed?" Angela's dad said.

The girls screamed again.

Her mom raised her eyebrows. "Why are you so jumpy?"

"'Cause first Brian scared the bejeebers out of us – then you did!"

Brian laughed. "Yeah, they screamed like little girls."

Angela crossed her arms. "That's because we *are* little girls!"

"Oh, yeah, that's right." Brian said. "But it was pretty funny."

"Maybe so," their mom said, "but it wasn't a nice thing to do."

"Especially since it's our first time sleeping in the treehouse." Angela said.

"You're right. I'm sorry," Brian said.

Angela's mom sent Brian to the house so the girls could calm down and settle in.

"Boys," Angela said in a huff.

"Yeah…boys," Jeannie agreed with a firm nod.

Brian walked backwards toward the house. "Hey, Angie!"

Angie yelled out the small window facing the house. "Yeah?"

"It is a cool treehouse!" He said and walked to the house.

"Thank you!"

On the way up the steps, Brian yelled out again, "Hey, Angie!"

"Now what?"

"It *was* pretty funny!" He laughed and went into the house.

Angela let out a deep sigh. "Brothers."

"Teenagers," her mom said, shaking her head.

Jeannie climbed on top of her sleeping bag and covered up with her blanket. "You guys wear me out," she said, sinking her head into her fluffy flowered pillow.

Angela grabbed the ropes to raise the ramp but then stopped.

"What's wrong?" her dad said.

"What happens if somebody, like Brian, plays a trick on us by locking us inside the treehouse with the outside latches and we can't get out?"

"That's a good question," he said. "I'll make a trap door in the floor for you to use as an escape hatch in case of an emergency. That will make everyone feel safer."

"That's a cool idea! Thanks, Dad."

Overflowing with joy, Angela scooted halfway down the ramp and wrapped an arm around each of her parents' necks. She grunted as she hugged them tight.

"Thank you, again, for my treehouse," she said.

"You're welcome. We're glad you like it," her mom said.

Her parents mashed a goodnight kiss into each of Angela's cheeks with a loud smack. She loved getting caught between her parents' kisses. Angela climbed back inside the treehouse and grabbed the ropes to raise the drawbridge.

"Ready?" her dad said.

"Ready!" Angela called.

"Raise the drawbridge!"

Angela pulled the ropes hand-over-hand until the heavy door fell into place, then latched it shut. "Got it!" she said.

"Good job," her dad said. "Goodnight, and have fun!"

"Have fun, but get some sleep," her mom said through the door.

"Goodnight!" the girls replied. "We will!"

Before lying down, Angela watched through the small window as her parents strolled hand in hand toward the house. It made her happy knowing how much they loved each other – and how much they loved her.

"Thank you, Mom, and Dad! I love you!" she called out.

"You're welcome! We love you, too!"

Angela closed the window part way, slithered into her sleeping bag and nestled her head into her pillow. It had been a long but good day and she was ready for sleep.

Angela's mom squeezed her husband's hand and smiled gently at the muffled sound of the girls' talking and giggling.

"Today was a good day," she said.

Her husband smiled and put his arm around her shoulders and gave her a squeeze.

"It sure was," he replied.

CHAPTER 10

Learning the Hard Way

The bright yellow rays of the waking sun shone through the leaf-covered branches of the tall oaks surrounding the treehouse. The sunbeams danced through the window and tapped on the girls' eyelids as if to say, *Good Morning. It's time to rise and shine!*

Angela rubbed her eyes and squeaked while she stretched herself nearly as long as her sleeping bag. Jeannie rolled onto her belly and hugged her pillow to watch Angela's morning stretch. Then Angela unlatched the door and lowered it into place, welcoming the beautiful *Sun-day* morning inside. The girls had just snuggled back into their sleeping bags when they heard someone whistle loud from Jeannie's house next door.

"That's my dad calling me home for breakfast," Jeannie said. "Coming!" she called back. "We're going to my grandparents' house in Minnesota today," she told Angela.

The girls worked fast to roll up their sleeping bags and tuck their few belongings into their pillowcases. Once outside, they lifted the drawbridge into place and latched it closed. Then Jeannie hurried through the ferns toward home, and Angela hurried up the path to the house to get ready for church.

"Thanks for coming over. It was fun!" Angela said.

"Thanks for having me over! Have fun decorating!" Jeannie hollered, swinging her pillow through the air as a wave goodbye.

"Thanks, I will!" Angela replied.

Angela liked going to church, just not this Sunday. Ideas for decorating the treehouse danced in her head, making her giddy with excitement. Her mind drifted repeatedly to the treehouse. Her pastor's words seemed to drone on forever. Angela crossed her arms and rested her chin on her chest. This is like a never-ending sermon, she thought. Her eagerness to work on the treehouse made it hard to sit still. Sometimes her legs swayed back and forth in quick, short movements; other times they jiggled up and down, making the pew her family was sitting in vibrate. Occasionally her mom reached over and placed her hand on Angela's thigh, which meant – sit still and pay attention. Each touch brought Angela's legs to a halt and the vibrations ceased. But a few minutes later, the jiggling would resume until the next touch on her thigh.

The sermon was finally over, and the pastor was finishing it up with a short prayer.

"Amen" was about the only thing Angela heard him say that day, but church wasn't over yet. There was always one last song while the pastor waited for someone to come forward for prayer. The congregation stood to their feet. At least now, Angela's jiggling wouldn't shake the pew... and everyone in it. She swayed gently to the beat of the music while mouthing the lyrics of the familiar song. Her mind ran through the final countdown... *verse one – chorus – verse two – chorus – chorus again*. Angela looked at the floor and tapped her toes impatiently, then she exhaled a big sigh and thought, *this song is also never-ending! Here we go again – repeat verse one – chorus – chorus – chorus again*. Then, like a running back awaiting the quarterback's Down-Set-Hut-Hut cadence, Angela was ready to make a run for the door. She gripped the pew in front of her and thought, *one last amen from the pastor and I'm outta here*.

"Amen," the pastor said after his final closing prayer. But what Angela heard was, Hike! The ball had been snapped and Angela was making a break for the door. "I'll meet you at the car!" she told her mom and dad.

"Get Sarah and Matt from the nursery first," her mom said.

"Okay!" Angela said. She didn't mind fetching her little brother and sister, especially if it meant getting home sooner.

Angela tucked her Bible in one arm like a football and wormed her way through the crowd like a full-back running through a sea of defenders. She was focused on the goal, saying, "Excuse me. Hello. I'm fine. Excuse me please," to all the friendly people along the way. Angela was like a well-shaken bottle of soda pop on a hot summer day – she was bursting with excitement.

The pastor reached out to shake Angela's hand, but she was in too big of a hurry for a handshake. She just smiled and waved to him on her way by, saying, "See you next week, Pastor Dan!"

Angela's parents were *not* in a hurry. They meandered through the crowd greeting friends until they stood before Pastor Dan.

"You'll have to excuse Angela," her dad said, shaking his hand. "She's in a hurry to get home and decorate her new treehouse."

"Oh...so that's why she's in such a rush," he said. "Good for her. I had a treehouse when I was a kid. I hope she likes hers as much as I liked mine."

Just then, Pastor Dan spotted Angela as she was about to dart out the door with Sarah and Matt in tow.

"Hey, Angela!" the pastor said. "Have fun with your treehouse!"

"Thank you!" Angela said, then she hurried the kids out the door and to the car.

Her parents smiled and waved to their pastor one last time before leaving.

After church, Angie's family enjoyed lunch at one of their favorite restaurants along the river. As was the kids' usual way after ordering, they looked out the large windows overlooking the river to watch for river life. They loved seeing the eagles ride the airwaves, floating in lazy circles high above the river. Today they were lucky enough to see an eagle swoop down and snatch a fish from the water with its long, sharp talons.

The kids were amazed by how quickly the eagle returned to the sky, even under the weight of its tightly held catch. They watched as the eagle flew off toward its nest, where it likely had a family of its own to feed. Then the kids returned to the table that was now covered with different sized plates of food. They told their parents all about the eagle they had seen.

"I can't wait to decorate the treehouse," Angela said.

"Can we help you?" Sarah asked.

"Sure, you can. We'll do it when we get home."

"They can help after their nap," her mom said.

Sarah and Matt's smiles quickly turned upside-down.

Angie said. "I'll get things ready, and then you can help me when you wake up."

That turned their frowns right-side-up again.

When they got home, Sarah and Matty went down for their nap without an argument. They knew the faster they went to sleep, the sooner they got to help Angie. Their dad put on his work clothes and went outside to build the trap door into the treehouse floor, while Angela's mom curled up in her favorite chair to enjoy a quiet afternoon of reading – and maybe a little nap.

There was no napping for Angela. She was on a scavenger hunt, searching the house for things to make her treehouse fun and comfortable. She found a battery-powered lamp in their camping equipment, and some throw pillows in the playroom, along with some other do-dads from here and there, which she stacked by the back door. Occasionally Angela's mom looked up from her book and smiled as she watched Angela scurry by.

"Do we have a rug or something soft for the floor so it's more comfortable?" Angela asked her mom.

"Hmm. I don't know. Let me think about that."

Then Angela had an idea. "I think I have a string of battery powered Christmas lights in my closet to hang on the ceiling like a nightlight. They'll look like stars. I'll be right back!" Angela hurried quietly up the stairs. She didn't want to wake the little ones. She pulled open her closet door and was met by a wall of stink.

"Whew! What is that smell?" Angela said out loud.

A putrid stench spewed from within, nearly making her hair stand on end. It almost smells as bad as the skunks, Angela thought. It smelled like…. Angela sniffed the air again. "Rotten eggs!" she said aloud. She suddenly remembered the uneaten lunch she did not remove from her backpack three weeks earlier when her mother told her to.

Angela hurried across the room and rummaged through her dresser drawers for her swimming nose plugs, hoping they would protect her nostrils from the horrid odor. She found them and clamped them tightly onto her nose. She was on a new mission, and it was more important than finding the Christmas lights.

Angela took a deep breath, then dug frantically through the mountain of dirty clothes, toys, and other stuff she'd mindlessly thrown into her closet instead of putting away.

"Oh, come on," she mumbled. By now Angela could taste the smell and removed the uncomfortable nose plugs. "Where is that backpack?" she growled. Frustrated, Angela began throwing everything backwards over her head. Finally, after tossing a few more things aside, she said, "There you are!"

Angela pulled the smelly backpack from the bottom of the closet, ripped the zipper open, and emptied its contents onto the now very messy floor. Angie found the half-eaten peanut butter sandwich right away. The once smooth-textured white bread was now a fuzzy, beautiful shade of dark green. It smelled rank but it was not the culprit. She pushed the backpack contents aside until she found the pungent source. She held in her hand a zippered plastic bag of

nasty, rotten, pink and beige tinted eggs that were now swimming the backstroke in a pool of milky colored liquid. The unappetizing contents looked like a school science project. "Gross! In the garbage you go!" So, Angela tiptoed down the stairs in her stocking feet as quiet as a mouse, in the hopes her mom wouldn't hear her or see the bags. But she forgot her mom could hear a tiny mouse all the way outside at the mailbox, *and* she seemed to have eyes in the back of her head!

Without looking up, her mom asked, "Did you find the lights?"

"Not yet. I'm still looking." Angela walked a little faster.

Her mom turned and looked at her. "What are you carrying – and *what is that smell?*"

Angela had been found out, and it was time to confess. "Well, remember when you told me to clean out my backpack on the last day of school?"

"Yes, I remember."

"Well… I didn't do it." Angela displayed the stinky bags. Now my bedroom stinks because of these rotten eggs!"

"Well, thanks to you, now the house smells like rotten eggs too."

"I know," Angie said. "I'm sorry."

"First of all, go put those nasty things in the garbage outside, then come back here so we can have a little talk."

"Yes, ma'am." Angela hung her head. She quickly disposed of the stinky bags, then returned and sat down beside her mom.

"I'm disappointed because you didn't obey my simple request," her mom said.

"Believe me, I'm sorry I didn't do like you told me to. I learned a *good* lesson."

"I'm sure you did, and I don't like doing this, but I think you're about to learn an even better lesson."

"I'm not going to like what's coming, am I?"

"No, you're probably not," her mom said. "But before I deliver your correction, you'll be happy to know that we do have a large piece of carpet left from the playroom that should be just about the right size for the treehouse. It's rolled up and standing in the corner downstairs. You're welcome to use it."

"Thank you," Angela said. "I'll get it later."

Her mom continued. "Now, for the other matter." Her mom spoke in a calm voice. "I appreciate your honesty, but... because of your disobedience you will not be decorating or playing in your treehouse today.

"You may first sit on your bed and read for thirty minutes, with your bedroom door closed." She knew Angela would fall asleep if she laid down to read, and then she wouldn't take the discipline as seriously as she should.

"But it stinks up there."

"I know it does, and it was kind of you to share it with the rest of us."

"But I hate to read."

"I know you do."

"Also, you may *not* use air freshener, open the window, or use anything else to cover the odor."

Her mom knew the smell wouldn't hurt Angela, but it *would* teach her an important lesson in doing what was right.

"When your thirty minutes of reading is over, you get to clean your room. That means your closet, under your bed, hanging up or folding and putting away any clean clothes, putting everything in its place, and taking your dirty clothes down to the laundry room."

"But that'll take all day!"

"Yes, it probably will."

Angela pouted and looked at the floor.

Angela's mom knew Angie liked to take shortcuts and hide things to get out of work, so she wagged her finger at Angela and said, "Don't think I won't check on you to see if you're doing a good job." She peered over her reading glasses at Angela to make sure her point was clear.

"One more thing," her mom said, "Sarah and Matt are not allowed to help you or play in your room for the rest of the day."

Angela agreed and stood up, thinking her mom was finished.

"Hold it." Her mom held up her hand. "I'm not finished."

Afraid of what else was coming, Angela returned to her seat.

"You also get to make your bed – with clean sheets, dust all your furniture, and then finish by vacuuming your room, every square inch, in every corner, under your bed, and in your closet. After all that is done, you may air out your room and spray air freshener to make it smell good again." Her mom paused. "Now I'm finished."

"Alright. I'll do a good job," Angie said. She hugged her mom. "I won't do that again," she said on her way up the stairs.

Just then, Sarah and Matt came out of their room.

"Hi, you guys! Did you have a good nap?" Angela said.

"Yep! We're ready to help you in the treehouse," Sarah said.

"Sorry, but Mom said I have to clean my bedroom today, so we'll have to decorate the treehouse tomorrow," Angie said.

The kids followed Angie to her room and sweetly offered to help her – that is, until they smelled her room.

"Pee-uuu!" Sarah pinched her nose. "It's stinky in here."

Matty pinched his little nose, saying, "Peee-uuu!"

The kids backed away from the doorway.

"Your room is stinky and messy," Sarah said. "We're gonna play downstairs."

Angie snickered. "That's why I have to clean my room. We'll decorate tomorrow."

Angela surveyed the unpleasant situation from her doorway, "Sarah's right. It *is* stinky and messy in here," she said to herself. At that, Angela reached deep within herself for a strong dose of determination. She drew in the last breath of fresh air she would get for a while, stepped into her bedroom, and pulled the door closed behind her. "Just get it done!" she told herself.

If Angie had to read, she wanted to read something with adventure. She didn't have many books in her room, but among those on the shelf were several older mystery series novels of The Sugar Creek Gang and Nancy Drew. Angela selected *The Sugar Creek Gang: The Mystery Cave* and sat on her bed. Angela had always wanted to read it, but the thick layer of dust on the top was evidence to the contrary – that never happened. Angela wiped away the dust, looked at her clock and began reading. Before long, a *tap-tap-tap* on Angela's door interrupted her reading.

Angela's mom opened the door a few inches. "It's awfully quiet up here," she said through the narrow opening.

"You can come in," Angela said. She forgot about the lingering rotten egg smell that her nose had become familiar with.

"Your room smells *eggs-traordinary*, so I'll stay right here. What have you been doing all this time? Your room is a disaster!"

"I know… but you told me I had to read for thirty minutes first."

"I know I did, but thirty minutes was up forty-five minutes ago."

"What!" Angela looked at the clock. "I can't believe I've been reading for more than an hour! I can't stop reading this book." She showed the book's front cover to her mom.

"Well, you can stop for now," her mom said, her eyes shifted across the floor. "Because, from the looks of things, you have your own adventure to pursue right here – and your closet is the Mystery Cave." Then she spoke in a mysterious voice, "Who knows what lost treasures you'll discover in there." Switching to her normal "mom" voice, she said, "Okay, enough playing around. Get started, and I'll check on you later."

"Yes, Mom." Angela tore a strip from a school paper to mark her place in the book.

Her mom scrunched her face and fanned the smell away with her hand. "I'm going downstairs before this smell takes the curl out of my hair!"

Angela giggled and returned the book to its home on the shelf. Apparently, her nose was now used to the prolific eggy perfume lingering in her room. She worked non-stop for an hour, first decluttering the top of her dresser and chest of drawers, since that was the easiest task. Next, she dealt with the overwhelming mess she'd thrown from her closet, and what was still in her closet. Then she hung-up and folded any clean clothes, putting them where they belonged; her dirty clothes she threw into her hamper. Angela struggled, but somehow transported her heaping clothes hamper down two flights of stairs to the laundry room in the basement.

Angela's mom watched the mass of dirty clothes pass by and thought it best to begin washing the heap right away. So she went downstairs and taught Angela how to sort her clothes into two piles, light-colored and dark-colored, then how to load and run the washing machine. Angela returned to her adventure upstairs while the first load washed. It wasn't long before Angie had everything put away and the furniture dusted. She was on a roll!

Angela compacted her overflowing wastebasket with her foot. Then she lugged it down the stairs and emptied it into the large outdoor can by the garage. She walked back upstairs, swinging the now empty wastebasket as she went. With everything off the floor, she vacuumed every inch of her room and closet. She even laid on her belly and vacuumed under her bed.

Meanwhile, Angela's dad had finished the escape hatch, put his tools away, showered, and was ready for his Sunday afternoon nap. He laughed when his wife told him the *eggs-traordinary* tale, then he stretched out in his recliner and fell fast asleep.

Angela's mom smiled each time Angela hustled up and down the stairs for one thing or another. After the whirring sound of the vacuum stopped, the next sound she heard was Angela spraying air freshener in her room and in her closet. Her room was so neat and clean it almost sparkled!

Angela took one last look around her room, then proudly announced to her mom, "My room is ready for inspection!"

"Wow! Is this the same room? It even smells good!"

Angela's mom looked around the room, then ran her fingers along the furniture to see if Angela really had dusted well. She looked at her dust-free fingers and gave Angela her nod of approval. Then her mom got down on her hands and knees to check under the bed. To her amazement, it was as "clean as a whistle." Fully expecting to find the dresser drawers in their usual disarray – they were surprisingly neat. Of course, most of Angie's clothes *were* in the laundry. Her mom smiled and nodded again. Now, just one last place to check. Angela's mom placed her hand on the closet doorknob.

"Do I dare look in the Mystery Cave?" she asked.

"Go ahead," Angela said. She was confident of receiving her mother's approval.

Her mom opened the door and smiled. "Impressive! Clean. Neat. Fragrant – and in a good way this time. Good job, Angie!"

"Thanks, Mom. You know, I never thought I'd be happy about cleaning my closet, but I found all kinds of good stuff in there. I found the Christmas lights I was looking for, and some more stuff for my treehouse. Plus, I found some things I'd been missing for a long time, like the key for my skateboard wheels, my sketch pad, one of my favorite shoes, and my swim goggles."

"Good. Now you have just enough time to take a shower before supper. You need to be clean, neat, and fragrant like your room."

Angela laughed. "That's a good idea."

While Angela showered, she thought of how good it felt to have a clean room. She couldn't wait for her dad to see it after supper... even though she wasn't proud of why it was so clean.

Angela's dad was shocked when he saw her sparkling room. He couldn't believe what he saw, saying, "Your mom was right; your room looks incredible!" Then he said in his punny, corny humor, "I understand, your room smelled quite *eggs-traordinarily fowl* this afternoon." Switching to his dad tone, he told Angela, "I'm sure you know that if you had done what your mother told you to do, this wouldn't have happened."

"I know. I promise I'll do better."

"I think you learned a good lesson today – the hard way."

"Believe me...I learned a very good lesson. The funny thing is – first Mom punished me by making me read, because she knows I hate to read. But now I want to go to bed early so I can read, and hopefully finish the story."

Angela's dad put his hand on her forehead. "Are you okay? Are you ill? Maybe you have a fever."

"Very funny!" Angie said. "The story's really good and I want to see how it ends."

"I never expected to hear those words cross your lips," he said. "You may go to bed whenever you're ready." Her dad gave her a tight hug, and said, "I'm proud of you for doing such a good job."

Sarah and Matty got to play with Angela in her room until their bedtime. Then Angela brushed her teeth, changed into her pajamas, and switched on her bedside lamp. Angela was surprised at how eager she was to pluck the book from its shelf and crawl into her freshly made bed to read. So, at just 8:30 p.m., Angie snuggled into her clean bedding and rejoined the Sugar Creek Gang's adventure.

Angela's parents tucked the little ones into bed, then came to tell Angela goodnight, standing at each side of her bed. Her dad looked around the clean room once more.

"We still can't believe how clean your room is," he said.

"We're very proud of you," her mom said. "Thank you, also, for being such a wonderful big sister to Sarah and Matty. They love you very much."

"Thank you," Angela said. "I love them, and I love you both." Angie hugged and kissed each of them on the cheek.

"Goodnight, Honey. I love you," her mom said.

"I love you, too, Sweetie," her dad said. "Goodnight."

Her dad stopped before going out the door and said, "I never thought I'd say this, but don't stay up too late reading."

Angie smiled, and said, "Okay, I won't."

Her dad smiled, then flicked off the ceiling light and closed the door partway behind him.

Angela's bedside lamp provided a nice glow to read by. She snuggled into her pillow and looked around her glistening room. As much as she liked the way it looked, and if she were honest, she knew it wouldn't stay that way for long. She turned her eyes back to the pages, and before long she drifted off to sleep.

Before turning in for the night, Angela's mom returned to her daughter's room to check on her. Angela was sound asleep with the book on her chest. Her mom grinned and carefully slid the book from Angela's hands so as not to wake her, then kissed her on the head and turned out the lamp.

Her mom could now go to bed feeling content. She knew that discipline, though unpleasant at the time, was a necessary part of life, and it had turned out to be a good day after all.

Angela awoke early the next morning. She was eager to decorate the treehouse and try out the new trap door. After breakfast, the three kids carried all the items Angie had stacked by the door down the path to the treehouse. As usual, Angie led the way with Matty close behind her and Sarah in the rear – each carrying what they could handle. They were like Snow White and the *two* dwarfs. They worked happily together throughout the morning. They would have whistled while they worked if they knew how.

Sarah and Matty waited by the ramp while Angela checked out the escape hatch in the floor. It opened like a door with a pull-ring. When she opened the hatch she thought, *this would be a fun way to sneak out and trick someone or scare them.* So, Angela lowered herself feet first through the opening, and pulled the door closed behind her. Then he crawled out from under the treehouse and jumped to her feet by the kids.

"Ta-da!" she said. "That is *so* cool! Let's decorate!"

Angela rolled the carpet into place first thing so it was easier on their knees when they crawled around, and to hide the escape hatch. She hoped the carpet, and the little kids, would keep the trap door a secret, at least for a while. Next, Angela covered most of the ceiling with the large movie posters she'd collected. Sarah was just the right height to hold the posters up while her big sister secured them in place with the push pins Matty handed her, using her new hammer (*or hammuw, as Matty would say*) to tap them in. Then she used small hooks to string the Christmas lights across the ceiling.

"Let's see how it looks," Angie said, then flipped the switch turning on the lights.

"Yay!" The kids shouted and clapped their hands.

"The lights are so pretty!" Sarah said.

"That looks great!" Angela said. "Let's do the walls now."

They covered the walls with more posters and magazine pages of Angela's favorite movie stars, singers, and bands.

"Hey, kids! Time for lunch!" their mom hollered from the porch.

"We'll be right there!" Angela replied.

The three busy bees were ready for a lunchbreak after buzzing about the treehouse all morning.

Angela put the remaining touches on the treehouse after a tasty lunch while the little ones napped. She placed a small black metal table beneath the window on the back-end wall for the lamp and a small, old-school battery-operated radio that was her mom's when she was a teenager. The table was from her grandfather's very first flower shop in 1960. Then Angela scattered the pillows and other items around the treehouse, with the finishing touch being a small autographed pillow bearing the image of her favorite heart-throb action star... Brian's favorite thing to tease her about.

Up from their nap and ready to help, Sarah called out from the porch, "Here we come, Angie!" They toddled down the path to Angie's welcoming smile and open arms.

Angela pointed to the treehouse. "Look. I think it's finished."

She crossed her arms and admired their handiwork. Sarah and Matt mimicked their big sister by doing the same thing. Angela was beaming with joy.

"Job well done," Angela said. "Thank you for helping."

"You're welcome," replied Sarah and Matty.

The three kids played in the treehouse until suppertime.

A few days later, Angela's mom thought of a way to easily make a teeter-totter for the kids with some of the long leftover boards. She attached two sturdy boards across two trees closely spaced and near the treehouse with some long nails. Then they slid a long, wide board between the two cross-boards and anchored it into place with two strong hinges on each side. Her mom screwed a handle to each end so the kids could hold on tight while playing. It worked! Within an hour the kids had a teeter-totter.

Many days, Angela and her friends bumped, balanced, and sailed up and down on the teeter-totter. Angie, being twice Sarah and Matt's combined size, sat Sarah and Matt together on one end while she rode on the other, being careful to teeter just enough to make it fun, but safe for them.  The teeter-totter wasn't fancy, it was just simple, old-fashioned fun.

The treehouse was Angela's special place. It could be whatever she and her friends imagined it to be. One day the treehouse might be a fort in the wild west under attack by the enemy; a castle with a drawbridge across a crocodile-filled moat surrounding it; or it could be a tunnel leading through a cave of bats to hidden treasure.

Angela especially liked using the treehouse's trap door in one of her great adventures. It could be the hatch door to a submarine submerging to the depths of the ocean in search of a giant sea creature; or a hatch door between compartments in a spaceship on its way to Jupiter, Mars, or a distant galaxy. She could pretend the hatch was a large stone covering a secret tunnel she had dug to escape the dungeon that held her captive. The possibilities were as endless as Angela's imagination.

Some of Angela's favorite times were when she had one or two friends sleepover in the treehouse. Her mom would often build them a small campfire for roasting hot dogs or marshmallows for s'mores. Angela's dog Casey kept her company on days when she played by herself; he often slept beside her to make her feel safe on nights when she slept in the treehouse alone.

Many days Angela and her friends played games in the treehouse while listening to music on her little radio and hung out on the teeter-totter and the open drawbridge talking and laughing. Angela even liked spending rainy days in her treehouse. She enjoyed the pitter-patter sound of a soft rain on the treehouse roof, but if it stormed, she stayed safely indoors playing her favorite video games, watching television or a good movie, and playing with Sarah and Matty. She could always find *something* fun to do!

One day Angela got a grand idea for one more special thing – something she could enjoy by herself, or with someone – one more big thing to ask her parents for.

CHAPTER 11

Not Just *Any* Swing

Angela was thrilled with her new treehouse and teeter-totter, but something was missing - something that every kid would like to have – a tire swing. One day, while hanging out in her treehouse, Angela had a conversation with her dog Casey. As usual, she had his full attention; he was a good listener.

Angela stroked Casey's head, saying, "I wish I had a tire swing; the little kids could play on it too," she told him. "It shouldn't cost very much since Dad works for a tire company. I bet an old tire would be cheap... maybe even free. I'll ask Dad tonight," she said. "What do you think, Casey? Wouldn't that be fun?"

Evening came, and the family sat down together for dinner.

"What did you do today, Angie?" her dad said.

"Mostly, I hung out in my treehouse with Casey." Then she thought, *now is the time to ask for a tire swing.* "Hey Dad, you know I love my treehouse, but do you think you could get an old tire from work and make a tire swing for us kids to play on?"

"Yes, I think so," he said. "I loved having a tire swing when I was a kid. Tomorrow I'll check and see what the guys in the tire shop have."

"Thanks, Dad!" Angela said.

Her mom grinned and said in a curiously sly way, with a gleam in her eyes, "Guess what?"

Angela knew her mom's eyes sparkled like that when she had a brilliant or clever idea, so she was intrigued by her mom's tone.

"I just learned how to build a terrific tire swing on a DIY *(Do It Yourself)* show last week," she said. "And when I say terrific, I mean *super – duper – deluxe – out of this world* – tire swing!"

"Wow! Let's build it!" Angela said.

"You don't even know what it looks like," her dad said.

"Hey – if Mom says it's terrific, it *has* to be terrific."

"I'll draw a picture of what I saw after supper," her mom said.

Angela was filled with delight and hurried to her bedroom as soon as she finished eating. She quickly returned with a pencil and the sketch pad she found when cleaning her closet.

Angela took her mom's dinnerware to the kitchen to make room for her to draw. The whole family watched as she sketched the most amazing tire swing they'd ever seen. She explained how to build it as she drew.

"You were right," her dad said. "That's not just *any* tire swing... it's incredible!"

"That's the best tire swing ever!" Angela said. "Can we build it?"

"Here we go again," her dad said. "*First*, we need to see if we have a good place to hang it. *Second*, I need to see about getting the tires. And *third*, we have to take measurements and calculate what other materials we will need. Then we *might* be able to build it in a week or so." Then he said again before Angela got too excited, "We *might* get to...."

It was no use, Angela was over the moon with excitement for the tire swing. "Oh, boy! I can't wait!" she said, bouncing up and down on her chair. To Angela, MIGHT meant YES.

Friday came and Angela had but one thing on her mind – the tire swing. Her mom purchased the supplies for the super-duper extra fancy fantabulous tire swing earlier that week – screws, nuts, bolts, washers, hefty shiny silver chain, and a heavy-duty swivel hook for it to hang from. All they needed now were the tires.

Angela waited on the front porch steps for her dad to get home from work. He was later than normal, and patience was not one of her strengths. Twenty minutes had passed, and still no sign of him. She hopped to her feet and ran inside.

"Mom, can I call Dad to see what's taking so long?"

"Don't worry. He just called," her mom replied. "Something held him up at work, and he's on his way home."

"Okay. I'm going back outside to wait for him!"

Angela hurried outside and waited for her dad at the end of the driveway. In the meantime, she hummed a few tunes; redirected some wandering ants with a small stick; pitched some pebbles at a tree; and even tied her shoes. Suddenly, she heard a car coming down the street and looked up.

"Hi, Dad!" Angela yelled, waving her arms above her head.

Angela ran after his car when he pulled into the driveway and greeted him with a bear hug.

"What took you so long?" she said.

Without saying a word, her dad motioned for her to follow him to the back of the car. He pressed a button on his key fob and the trunk popped open revealing a cargo of black gold. He had four beautiful black tires stacked neatly in the trunk, and two more standing on the floor in the back seat of his car.

"Thank you, thank you!" she said, hugging him again.

"You're welcome," he said. "You know… I think I'm as excited about the swing as you are. Let's take the tires to the backyard."

Her dad carried one tire in each hand, but the tires were too heavy for Angela, so she rolled her tire. They made one more trip with the three remaining tires. Angela and her dad talked about the cool tire swing on the way back to the house.

Suddenly he said, "Angie, there's something on your nose!"

Alarmed, Angie said, "What is it?" She grabbed her nose and rubbed it. "Did I get it?"

"Now it's on your cheek!" he said, pointing to her left cheek.

Angela slapped her cheek and rubbed it hard. "Did I get it?"

"I think you got it that time," her dad said.

"I hope so!" Then Angie rubbed both cheeks and all around her face. "Oooo… that made my whole face crawl!" Then she scratched and rubbed her neck. "That creeped me out!"

Her dad tried hard not to laugh. He knew there was nothing on her face before, but now there was. Their hands were as black as charcoal from the tires, and now Angela's face was too. They raced up the back steps and into the house for supper. Angela's mom noticed Angie's blackened face and their filthy hands right away.

"Whoa!" her mom said. "You two go wash your hands before you do anything else, and don't touch *anything* on the way."

They looked at their filthy hands and smiled. "Yes, ma'am!" they said, then they stood up tall, saluted her, and marched to their separate bathrooms.

"Angela," her mom said, "you may want to look in the mirror."

"How come?"

"You'll see." Her mom chuckled to herself.

Then Angela saw her reflection and knew why. "Hey! That was a dirty trick!" she hollered to her dad.

"Yep, it was," he hollered back, "and you fell for it."

At dinner, the family enjoyed hearing about the dirty trick he played on her. Everyone, including Angela, laughed.

Angela struggled to sleep that night, knowing tomorrow was tire swing day. She punched and scrunched her pillow; she flipped and flopped and, finally, was overcome by sleep.

Saturday dawned with glorious sunshine. Angela awakened a little later than normal. She rubbed her eyes, performed her usual morning stretch routine, then she sat up on the edge of her bed. The house was unusually quiet. *No bacon cooking? Did I oversleep? Did everyone oversleep?* she wondered. Angela looked at her clock and shrieked, "8:23!" She climbed into her grubby clothes, and sprinted downstairs. The house was empty.

Angela called out, "Mom? Dad? Where is everybody?"

Her mom stepped out of her bedroom. "Good morning. What are you yelling about?"

"I thought everyone was gone, but me," Angela said.

"Brian's at work, and your dad took Sarah and Matty with him to buy doughnuts for breakfast. You know how they love going to the bakery for their favorite doughnuts with sprinkles."

"I hope Dad remembers my chocolate long johns."

"Don't worry. He knows," her mom said. "Let's eat outside on the picnic table since it's a beautiful morning. We'll get everything on the table so we're ready to eat when they get back. You set the table with plates, napkins, and glasses. I'll make the coffee, and you put out the milk and orange juice.

"Okey-dokey!" Angie gathered everything except the milk and juice and quickly set the table. Then she grabbed the jug of milk and the orange juice from the fridge and took them outside.

Angela's dad and the kids returned with the doughnuts a few minutes later and joined them at the picnic table. Her dad carried a boxed assortment of carb-loaded sugary goodness; Sarah and Matt each carried their own small white bakery bag, with each containing a doughnut covered with colorful sprinkles.

"Boy, it's a good thing we have all day to work off this sugar," her mom said.

Smiling, Angie said, "Yeah!" Then she sunk her teeth into the gooey chocolate iced long john.

Not having one tree large enough for the massive tire swing, Angela's parents would have to hang it from a large beam between two trees to support its weight. After breakfast, Angela's dad went to the lumberyard to buy the beam, while Angie's mom cleared the picnic table, and Angela got the little kids set up with their toys on the large back porch.

It wasn't long before Angela's dad returned with a huge, ten-foot-long beam. Her parents each hoisted one end of the heavy beam onto a shoulder and carried it to the backyard, while Angela played with Sarah and Matty. Then, armed with tools and supplies, Angela and her parents began to build the very best tire swing ever.

Angela's parents attached the heavy beam about eight feet high between two strong trees near the treehouse. They used some long bolts, along with steel cable to secure each end to the trees, since it had to support the weight of the swing and up to five kids. Then they attached the heavy-duty swivel-hook to the bottom side of the beam, so the tire swing would turn freely while swinging.

With that done, it was finally time to construct the swing. Angela's mom and dad laid the first two tires, one on top of the other, across a pair of sawhorses. Those tires would be the hub, or center of the swing, holding it all together. Then they bolted the four remaining tires, upright and evenly spaced, to the first two tires. Angela's excitement grew with the addition of each tire.

"This really is going to be the best tire swing ever!" Angela said. "I can't wait until it's finished! How much longer?"

"Be patient," her dad said. "We have more to do before it's ready to ride on, but we're getting close."

Angela knew their hard work would pay off, but that didn't make the time go by any faster.

Finally, her dad said, "The tires are bolted together. Now it's time to attach the chains so we can hang it."

Her mom and dad measured and cut the heavy chain into four equal lengths. Then they threaded each length of chain through one of the four outside tires and secured them together at the top with one large connecting link.

"Is it finished?" Angela asked. "Can we hang it now?"

"Yes, it's finished," her mom said with a smile. "Let's hang it!"

Angela got the job of hooking the chains on the hook when her parents lifted the mass of tires into position. She climbed the ladder and held onto the beam to steady herself. Then she grasped the chains with both hands while her parents positioned themselves on each side of the swing and got a secure hold of the bottom tire.

"We'll lift on the count of three," her dad said. "Ready... One, two, three, L-I-F-T." Her mom and dad growled like bears when they lifted the swing into place.

"Quick! Put the top link onto the hook!" her dad told Angela.

Angela placed the bundle of heavy chains on the awaiting hook and quickly pulled her hands out of the way.

"It's on!" she shouted.

Her parents lowered the mass till it hung by its shiny chains.

Angela climbed down the ladder and stared in awe at the beautiful masterpiece they had built.

"Now can I go for a ride?" she asked.

"Just a minute," her mom said. "Let's make sure it's safe."

Standing on opposite sides of the swing, her parents took hold of the chains and stepped up with a foot in each tire on their side and bounced up and down a few times.

"That feels very sturdy," her mom said, stepping down.

"It sure does," her dad said. Then he stepped down and gave the swing a big push. When it swung back, he pushed it again, making it spin. He smiled wide and watched it swing back and forth several times before bringing it to a stop.

Satisfied, her dad said, "Okay, Angie. Take it for a ride."

Angela gripped the two closest chains, gave the swing a push to get it started, and stepped up, placing her feet in two of the tires.

"I can't believe I have a super-duper tire swing!" she hollered.

Angela pulled on the chains and pushed with her feet to coax the swing higher. Her mom and dad helped by giving the swing one more giant push. Now she was really feeling the wind on her face.

"This is great!" Angela said. "Spin it, Dad!"

"Here you go!" Her dad pushed hard and sent the swing in a clockwise spin to the right.

"Woo-hoo! This is great! Thank you, Mom, and Dad!"

Angela's joy tanks were full. She couldn't help but smile wide as she rode the swing back and forth, 'round and 'round.

"I can't wait to tell my friends about my new swing!" she said. "Can I ask them to come over tomorrow to take the swing on its maiden voyage?"

"You sure can!" said her mom.

Again, Angela's parents beamed with joy as they gathered their tools and walked toward the house.

"It really is a cool tire swing," her dad said to his handy wife.

"It really is," she said. "Once again, we did a good job together."

Angela's dad smiled and said, "I would have been the envy of the neighborhood with a swing like that when I was a kid."

Angela soared back and forth on the swing until dinnertime.

"Angela! Come inside! Time for supper!" her mom called.

"Okay! I'll be right there!" Angela gave the swing a few more pushes with her legs, then crawled onto the center tire and flipped onto her back, her arms and legs sprawling in different directions. She closed her eyes, smiled, and rode the magnificent mass of black rubber until it slowed to a stop. *I can't wait to do this again tomorrow,* Angela thought. Then she jumped off the swing and gave it one good push before running to the house for supper.

CHAPTER 12

The Maiden Voyage

It was Sunday again, and Angela attended church with her family as usual. And, as usual, she had other things on her mind. Angela barely heard a word the pastor said. She pretended to pay attention on the outside, but on the inside, she was smiling as she thought about playing on her new super-duper tire swing. Then, again as usual, instead of going home after church, her family went out for lunch. Angela was impatient and couldn't sit still. Every few minutes she looked over her shoulder for their food to come.

"Why is this taking so long?" Angela whined.

"The food will be here soon," her mom said in a soft voice.

"But it's taking forever," Angela said.

"Your tire swing will be there when we get home," her dad said.

"Okay." Angela sighed, then propped her elbows on the table and plopped her chin into her hands. Sitting still wasn't easy for her. She was excited to play on the new tire swing with Jeannie, Jeremy, and Jay. Finally, their food arrived. Angela leaned over her plate and began gobbling up her food like she hadn't eaten in a week.

"Angela, slow down and breathe," her dad said. "We're not leaving until everyone has finished eating."

"Yes, sir." Angela said. She sat up a little straighter in her chair and tried to eat at a slower pace.

When everyone had finished eating, Angela said, "Can we go now?" She jiggled in her chair like she had ants in her pants.

"Yes. We can go now," replied her dad. "You and your mom take Sarah and Matt to the car while I pay the bill."

Angela helped fasten the little kids into their car seats and they were on their way. She rattled on and on about the tire swing and her friends the entire way home.

"Can I call Jeannie, Jeremy and Jay to see if they can come over to play on my swing?" she asked her mom when the car turned into their subdivision.

"You can call your friends after you change into play clothes and put your church clothes away," her mom said.

Then Sarah said, "We want to play on your swing too!"

"Everyone can play on the swing today," their mom said.

"Yay!" the kids exclaimed.

"Oh, boy! I can't wait for my friends to see my new swing! I'm sure they're gonna love it as much as I do!" Angela said.

It just so happened her friends were already outside, hanging out together at the end of the cul-de-sac. Angela waved and shouted to them through her open car window before her dad turned into their driveway.

"You guys wanna play on my new tire swing? It is *so-o-o* cool!"

"Yeah! We'll be right over!" they said.

"I'll be out after I change my clothes!"

Angela ran into the house and scurried up to her room.

"Remember to hang up your church clothes before you go out to play!" her mom said from the living room.

"Okay, I will!"

Angela changed her clothes and was back downstairs in record time. She shoved her feet into her shoes, grasped the doorknob, and told her mom, "I'm going outside now!"

"Did you hang up your clothes?" her mom said. She knew her daughter very well.

With her hand still grasping the doorknob, Angela hung her head and exhaled a frustrated sigh. Her mind raced as she quickly reasoned with herself. *I can lie and say yes, so I can go out and play and hang my clothes up later. Mom would never know. But what if Mom checks my room and finds out that I lied? Then I'll be in big trouble again. I'll be grounded for a week – maybe longer, and I won't get to play on my tire swing, in my treehouse, or with my friends.* Angela knew she needed to answer truthfully.

"No, I didn't. I'll do it right now," she said.

Angela chose to do what was right, to do what her mom had told her to do. She shuffled her feet back upstairs and put the clothes away she'd left lying on the floor. Then she flew back down the stairs with a clear conscience. Her mom met her at the door.

"Now can I go outside?" Angela asked.

"Yes," Her mom said, hugging her.

"Can you bring Sarah and Matt out after their nap?"

"I sure can. Have fun!"

"I'm coming, you guys!" Angela shouted, running down the path toward them.

The three friends were awe-struck by the enormous tire swing. They looked it over, turning it around and examining every detail. Jeannie, Jeremy, Angela and Jay were excited about the swing and were all talking loudly at the same time as they climbed aboard the swing. Then they heard a loud voice.

"THAT IS THE COOLEST TIRE SWING I HAVE EVER SEEN."

Everyone jerked their heads around to see who it was.

"Kelly!" everyone shouted. "Come join us!"

Angela, surprised to see their device-loving friend trotting down the path toward them, said, "What are you doing here?"

"I rode my bike down to see what you guys were doing and heard a commotion coming from your backyard," Kelly said. "It sounded like you were having fun, so I came to see what was up."

"C'mon, Kelly! Climb aboard!" Angela said. "We're taking my new super-duper tire swing on its maiden voyage!"

"Are you sure there's room?" Kelly asked.

"Sure! Come on!" they all shouted.

Jeannie, Jeremy, and Jay were already perched atop three of the four side tires, and Angie had dibs on the fourth one.

"You can lay in the middle tire," Jeannie said. "C'mon up!"

Happy to be included, Kelly climbed up, squeezed in between the chains, flipped onto his back, and held on. He didn't tell the others, but when he flipped over, his backend slipped into the hole and got... well, wedged.

"Kelly, you can take it easy and enjoy the ride while we do the work," Angela said. "We'll take turns riding in the middle."

Kelly chuckled. "We'll take turns if I can get outta here."

"Don't worry. We'll help you," Jay said.

"Alright. Let's see how this swing does with all five of us on it. I'll give it a big push, then climb on," Angela said. "Hold on tight!"

Kelly laughed and said, "Don't worry about me. I don't need to hold on tight... I'm tightly held, and I'm not going anywhere."

Everyone laughed. Thankfully Kelly had a sense of humor about his chunkiness!

Angela grabbed the bottom tire and pulled the swing toward her as far as she could, then pushed the fully-loaded mass as far as she could and climbed onboard, taking her seat on the remaining tire.

"Jay and I will push with our feet from this side, then, Jeannie and Jeremy, you push from your side. We should be able to get this thing swinging pretty high if we all work together."

"Aye, Aye, Captain," they answered.

The now Fearless *Fivesome* swung higher with each push and pull until they felt like they were soaring like the eagles.

After a while, Angela's mom brought Sarah and Matt out for their turn on the swing.

"Would you kids mind giving the little ones a turn?" she asked.

"No, we don't mind," Jeannie said.

"C'mon you guys, let's take a break," said Jay.

They let the swing slow down just enough to hop off.

Kelly tried to wiggle free while the swing swayed, but by now he was really lodged in the tire.

"Umm... you guys? What about me?" Kelly said. He was the only one still on the swing... or *in* the swing.

"I think I'm kinda... stuck here."

Everyone laughed, including Kelly.

"I'll help you," Jay said. He reached up and took hold of Kelly's hand. "One-Two-Three!" Jay grunted.

"I'm still here," Kelly said slowly.

"Let me get higher so I have better leverage," Jay said. So, he climbed onto the tires and again took Kelly's hand.

Angela braced Jay's back in case he fell when Kelly popped free.

"Again," Jay said, "One-Two-Three-PULL!" Jay grunted louder. But Kelly's backend didn't budge.

"I tell you... I'm stuck," Kelly said.

"Hang on," Jeremy said. "Let *me* help."

"What can you do?" Jeannie said. "You're not as strong as Jay."

"I'm not stronger," he said, "but weasel butts can go where others can't." Jeremy lay under the middle tires and placed his feet against Kelly's very wedged backside.

"Hey, what are you doing down there?" Kelly said.

"Uh, you wanna get unstuck, don't you?" Jeremy said.

"Absolutely!" Kelly said.

"Then, when I say 'go' Jay will pull, and I will push."

"Okay. I sure hope this works," Kelly said.

"Ready?" Jeremy said. "One-Two-Three-GO."

Kelly popped out of the tire like a cork from a bottle!

"Hey, it worked! Thanks, you guys! Let me know if I can ever repay the favor."

Jeremy said, "I don't think that'll ever happen."

"Why not?" Kelly asked.

Jeremy smirked and pointed to his backside. "Weasel butt!"

Everyone laughed loud, especially Kelly.

Angela climbed onto the swing and laid on her back in the center tire and prepared herself for the little kids to join her for a ride.

"Don't get stuck!" Kelly said. "Remember *my* dilemma."

Angela laughed. "I'll try not to," she said.

Angela's mom placed Sarah on one side of Angela, and Matty on the other. Angela held onto them, and they held onto the chains. Their mom pushed the swing easy at first, then gradually higher. Sarah and Matt's eyes and smiles got bigger with each push.

"Again! Again!" they shouted.

After a good ride, their mom said, "Come on you two. It's time to let the big kids play."

Then Angela told Sarah and Matty, "You guys can play with me anytime, so I'm gonna play with my friends for now, okay?"

Sarah and Matty were sad but agreed. Then they and their mom enjoyed watching the big kids swing before going inside to play.

The big kids laughed and talked and swung for hours. Each time someone different took their turn on the middle tire, they joked about not getting stuck in the hole like Kelly; all but "Weasel Butt" Jeremy who had to lay stiff like a board and hold tight so he didn't fall all the way *through* the hole. The friends took occasional breaks, hanging out on the treehouse drawbridge and teeter-totter to rest their arms and legs before boarding the swing for another ride.

Near dinnertime, Angela's dad whistled loud for her from the porch. She knew that sound, just like Jeannie and Jeremy knew the sound of *their* dad's whistle, which could be heard even when deep in the woods. Angela often tried to whistle like him, but she could barely whistle the regular *lip-puckering* way.

"Angie, time for supper!" he hollered. "Tell everyone goodbye, and then come wash up so we can eat!"

"Okay! Be right there!" Then Angela told her friends, "See you guys later. Thanks for coming over; that was so much fun!"

Everyone said their goodbyes and headed home. Angela ran to the house, and upstairs to wash her hands and face. Then she went to her room, grabbed a pencil, and put a check mark on item 14 of her Summer Adventure List. She studied the list, reading each item quickly out loud. A smile crossed her face when she thought about what she might do next. Then she hustled downstairs to have dinner with her family.

My Summer Adventure List

1. Go exploring in the woods

2. Skateboarding

3. Go Hiking and Camping

4. Watch tv — Play video games — Watch movies
   (only on rainy or super hot days)

5. Have a lemonade stand

6. Ride trail bike on the trails

7. Swimming and Tubing

8. Stay up late and sleep late

9. Ride my bike

10. Sleepovers with friends

11. Play on the Slip n Slide

12. Go Roller Skating at the rink

13. Ride horses at the Ritchie's farm

14. <u>BUILD A TREEHOUSE!!!</u>

Many days Angela swung alone on her tire swing – sometimes pretending she was the captain of a mighty sailing ship, crashing through the ocean waves. Other times she lay across the middle tire on her belly with her arms spread wide like one of the eagles she had seen soaring above the river.

Angela's treehouse took the cake. The tire swing was the frosting on the cake and the teeter-totter was the cherry on top! She couldn't have been happier. Every day was a good day to Angela, even if it rained, because she could always find *something* fun to do on her *Summer Adventure List*.

What will be Angela's next Great Adventure?

Angela learned some important lessons:

- Don't give up on your hopes and dreams.
- Determination and hard work help make dreams come true.
- Great imagination turns ordinary days into great adventures.
- Good friends help to make hard work fun.
- There is great value in doing what is right.
- True friends don't give up on you.
- Devices and online friends can't replace real friends.
- Appreciate what your parents do for you.
- A little person can do big things.
- Don't get your backside stuck in a tire swing!

The End

ABOUT THE AUTHOR – PAULA JO MCELROY

Angela's Great Adventures: The Treehouse is a fun adventure story based on the actual events of the author's step-daughter. Paula says, "Angela was all about having fun and doing what was not considered *normal* for a girl to do back then. Now, in this time of social media and electronics, neighborhoods and parks, once alive with the chatter of children playing and scattered with bicycles, now lie silent and deserted. My hope is that Angela's stories will inspire readers to *take a break from their devices – go outside and have fun, enjoy nature, get dirty, and find their own adventures!*"

Paula enjoys telling stories, especially those from real life. It's worth noting that, for the most part, what she knows about writing she learned between the ages of 8-14. She's a good example of using what she learned in school later in life as an adult. So, to her young readers, Paula says, *"You don't know **now**, what you'll need to know **later**. So do well in school **now**, you'll thank yourself **later**."*

Growing up in the heart of the Midwest in Normal, Illinois, Paula says she is anything but normal. "I loved being outdoors and it wasn't uncommon for me to have a bug in a jar, be climbing trees, hunting for crawdads and making a dam in the small creek behind our house, or playing sports with my older brothers and the boys in the neighborhood. It wasn't until well into writing Angela's story that I realized how much I was like her as a kid – just not as care-free and bold." Paula's goal is for *The Treehouse* to be the first in a series of *Angela's Great Adventures* books. And, though based on actual experiences, the author has made use of creative freedom for the sake of fun and interest. What is true is for you to decide!

After 23 years in Wisconsin, Paula and her husband, Don, now live in Clarksville, Tennessee. She is a homemaker and part-time writer, enjoys gardening and being active in her church. She has a blended family of two step-children and two children, seven grandchildren, and two great-grandchildren with another on the way. Growing up in a blended family herself, Paula simply considers them *a family*.

Paula is a hands-on, project-loving, manual labor type of gal. She learned her building and decorating skills, along with her humor, from her dad; her cooking, baking, sewing, and homecare skills from her mother and her grandmother. She likes power tools *and* dressing up – but would still rather build a house than clean one!

Paula considers herself an extroverted-introvert; she loves being with people, yet she is quite content being at home on her own. She hates coffee and the smell of it, but she'll take a good cup of tea and a beautiful scenic view any day!

Contact Paula via email at paulajomcelroy@gmail.com or visit her website at paulajomcelroy.com.

Made in the USA
Monee, IL
09 November 2024

69688523R00083